The Cats of Silver Crescent

The Cats of Silver Crescent

KAELA NOEL

Greenwillow Books
An Imprint of HarperCollins Publishers

The Cats of Silver Crescent
Copyright © 2024 by Kaela Noel

The text of this book is set in 13-point Adobe Jenson Pro.
Book design by Paul Zakris
Chapter opener illustrations by Jessica Roux

Library of Congress Cataloging-in-Publication Data

Names: Noel, Kaela, author.
Title: The cats of Silver Crescent / by Kaela Noel.
Description: First edition. |
New York : Greenwillow Books, an Imprint of HarperCollins Publishers, 2024. | Audience: Ages 8-12. | Audience: Grades 4-6. |
Summary: "While on a weeks-long visit to her aunt Verity's house, eleven-year-old Elsby discovers there is more to the cats living in the house next door than first meets the eye"— Provided by publisher.
Identifiers: LCCN 2023037270 (print) | LCCN 2023037271 (ebook) |
ISBN 9780062956002 (hardcover) | ISBN 9780062956026 (ebook)
Subjects: CYAC: Cats—Fiction. | Magic—Fiction. | Friendship—Fiction. |
Fantasy. | LCGFT: Animal fiction. | Novels.
Classification: LCC PZ7.1.N628 Cat 2024 (print) |
LCC PZ7.1.N628 (ebook) | DDC [Fic]—dc23
LC record available at https://lccn.loc.gov/2023037270
LC ebook record available at https://lccn.loc.gov/2023037271
24 25 26 27 28 LBC 5 4 3 2 1
First Edition

Greenwillow Books

For Lucy Rose

CHAPTER ONE

12½ Silver Crescent

The old wooden cottage was frosted with curls of peeling white paint, like a gingerbread house melting in the sun.

It was the last house on the dead-end street, and it sat in the middle of a wide lawn sparkling with raindrops from the storm that had just passed. The forest pressed up against it, thick and menacing. Elsby MacBride peered into the bank of trees, wondering how something so green could be so dark.

"Twelve-and-a-half Silver Crescent," said Elsby's mother, squinting from her phone to the metal numbers hammered beside the house's two front doors, which stood side by side. She turned off the car engine and stepped out. "This must be it. Aunt Verity's is on the right."

Elsby stuck her head through the window and sniffed. Earth after rain—it smelled like magic potions would, if they were real. She hopped out and straightened the wrinkled cotton skirt of her sundress, then grabbed her slightly battered straw hat. Next she picked up her Save the Manatees tote bag and put the straps firmly over her shoulder. It contained her most precious things.

"Wait a second. We have to roll up our windows in case it storms again," said her mother. "This thing can't get further destroyed. At least not on my watch."

"This thing" was the tiny two-door tomato-red sports car Elsby's mother was borrowing from her friend Dirk. It was what her mother called a "junk bucket," with paint patches, no working air-conditioning, and windows that had to be wrenched up and down with duct-taped knobs. The insides were bright-orange plush and smelled like pine air freshener.

The drive from New York City to Rhode Island had taken several hours. Elsby stretched, pushed her glasses back up the bridge of her nose, and cranked the passenger-side window shut. The last inch took both hands. Then she gently patted the low roof. It was the flip-phone version of a car, but Elsby was fond of it.

"Here goes nothing," said her mother, staring at the house. "Elsby, while you're here, listen to Great-aunt Verity—or Aunt Verity. Well, whatever she asks you to call her. Be good. And I'm sorry."

"It's okay," said Elsby, even though it wasn't. But she couldn't let her mother know that, not when she knew already how guilty her mother felt for leaving Elsby alone for several weeks with a great-aunt Elsby had only met twice before in her life.

Elsby's mother was an art curator, which meant she got to plan exhibitions at museums and galleries. She had been asked to curate a show in Los Angeles, but she wouldn't be paid until after the opening—and there wasn't enough money to bring Elsby along for the installation and launch. That was why Elsby was staying with her mother's aunt while strangers sublet their apartment in Brooklyn.

The house had a long, white front porch. The door on the right opened and out stepped a tall woman who looked as thin and cautious as a stray cat. She wore a long blue dress so plain it could have been a nightgown, but Elsby was pretty sure it wasn't. She seemed too formal to wear anything but real clothes outside. She had a pale, pinkish face with some faint wrinkles and very dark Atlantic-blue eyes. Her hair was in a swirly brown-and-white bun atop her head, like a frosted cinnamon roll.

Elsby had expected her great-aunt to wear glasses and a tweed jacket, and maybe carry a pickax. She was a professor of archaeology at a university, which was why she had the summer free to watch Elsby.

"Heather!" Elsby's great-aunt called out, arms spread wide. She was smiling a tight-lipped, small smile. "And dear Elisabeth."

Only teachers on the first day of school called Elsby by her full name. *Elisabeth* was rich with nicknames, like a freshly pruned bush bursting with new shoots—Ellie, Liz, Libby, Lisa, Betsy, Beth. . . .

But everyone was startled by the name *Elsby*, because Elsby herself had made it up.

Elsby's mother hurried to the porch and embraced Aunt Verity. "She still goes by Elsby," she said.

Elsby followed her mother up the splintering wooden steps and let her aunt briefly embrace her. She smelled like books and incense.

Aunt Verity smiled, taking a step back. "Well then. Welcome to Snipatuit. Come in, come in! You must be quite tired." She pushed open the door marked "12 ½."

The door on the left—marked "12"—was wreathed in cobwebs.

"Who lives there?" asked Elsby, staring at it.

"Ah." Elsby's aunt got a wistful expression. "It was once the home of my landlady, Rose Fairweather. Such a kind woman. She passed away back in March."

"I'm so sorry," murmured Elsby's mother.

"I didn't know her very well, but she was a good

landlady." Aunt Verity let out a sigh. "She had no close family. Two nieces are feuding over the house." Aunt Verity shook her head. "She died alone, sadly."

Elsby shivered. People died all the time—including inside her own large apartment building back in Brooklyn. But death was not so scary in the city. How could a ghost haunt a place teeming with so many *living* people? But here, at the very end of this quiet Rhode Island street, it was different.

"No need to worry about ghosts, my dear," said Aunt Verity, as though she had read Elsby's mind. "I haven't felt the presence of any around this house. Regardless, Rose would be the friendly sort of ghost."

A sudden wind puffed through the trees.

Aunt Verity began asking Elsby's mother something about luggage. Elsby peered at the dead landlady's side of the house. Its windows had frilly lace curtains—all closed—that appeared gray in the afternoon light.

A curtain on the second floor twitched.

Elsby stared at it.

"Who lives in the landlady's place now?" Elsby asked, interrupting the grown-ups' conversation.

"No one," said Aunt Verity. "It's completely empty."

Elsby looked at the windows again. All the curtains were still.

"Can I explore the yard?" said Elsby, taking a step back.

"Do you feel okay?" Her mother widened her eyes. "You look queasy."

"No, no, um, I just want to see the garden," said Elsby. Her heart was beating very fast. She was *sure* she'd seen the curtain move.

"All right." Her mother still looked worried, and Elsby regretted having said anything. "Keep your hat on, okay?"

Elsby had light skin that burned easily.

"I will," she said.

"And no going into the woods," her mother continued. "There are ticks, remember? Ticks that can make you sick. And don't climb any trees."

They couldn't afford an accident.

"I know, I know," said Elsby. She shifted her tote bag's straps. "I'll be careful. It's okay, don't worry."

"Have a good time!" Aunt Verity said brightly.

Elsby nodded politely. With one hand on the brim of her hat, she took off running.

CHAPTER TWO

The Garden

The garden behind the house was full of tangled, wild blooms: a pastel rainbow of shaggy rosebushes, stoplight-red poppies, big hollyhocks swaying with pinkish bells, and daisy bushes as wide as a city sidewalk. There were many more flowers whose names Elsby didn't know. There was a vegetable garden, too—or what looked like the remains of one. It was a large rectangle fenced with tall poles and thin netting. Elsby peered into it. Everything was overgrown and weedy and dripping with raindrops.

She decided not to think about the curtain moving—or whatever that had been. Probably just a breeze. Old houses were like that. Drafty.

Elsby pulled her notebook and pencil case out of her tote bag.

A garden. A whole garden! For several weeks it was hers, and it was full of things to observe and draw. It was like winning the lottery.

Elsby wandered the stone path between the roses. Skinny weeds with small, pink blossoms brushed past her ankles. Startled little birds fluttered from the bushes, and tiny invisible things shook the lower leaves and fled at her approach. The wind gusted.

Elsby felt someone watching her. She turned to look at the back of the house. Aunt Verity's windows were half open and rippling with curtains. All the ones on the right side—the dead landlady's—were shut tight and covered with shades or heavy drapes. Two dormer windows stuck out from the roof above the second floor like sleepy, heavily lidded eyes.

In front of Elsby was a large, flat rock. It was nestled in a clump of pink roses. Out of habit, Elsby scanned the ground for broken glass and trash—there were none—and then sank down onto the rock. It was already dry.

The sun was hot, but the ground smelled cool and fresh, and the rock was as warm as something alive. She pulled her hair off her neck, tying it in one of the scrunchies she always kept around her wrist. She had thick, heavy hair that had once been Goldilocks blond and was now darkening, winter after winter, to a leafy brown.

Elsby propped her notebook on her knees and opened

her case of pencils. She chose a dark blue one with a perfect point.

THE HOPE LIST

-I hope Mom stays safe on her trip
-I hope Aunt Verity is not too weird
-I hope whoever is subletting our apartment doesn't wreck our stuff
-I hope Mom gets a real job—NO MORE FREELANCING! ! !
-I hope I finally finish writing & drawing a novel
-I hope I see some animals that are not only squirrels

Thwack.

A brownish blur shot out from a nearby rosebush in a shower of yellowish-brown petals.

A squirrel?

Elsby gasped and dropped her notebook and pencil.

Not a squirrel.

A bunny!

A real, live bunny rabbit

Elsby jumped to her feet.

"Wait, bunny! I promise I won't hurt you," she called.

The bunny paused at the edge of the dark woods and turned to look back at her, its tiny nose wiggling.

"That's right," Elsby whispered, slowly shuffling toward

it. "See? I'm a friend. I love animals. I would never hurt you."

The magical-potion earthy scent was stronger by the edge of the woods. The long grass was thick and cool, and the leftover rain quickly soaked Elsby's skirt. She studied the rabbit, surprised at how curiously it looked back at her.

"I just want to draw you," she murmured.

Elsby's heart pounded. This was her first chance to do a real-life sketch of a wild animal that wasn't a squirrel or a pigeon—but her notebook and pencils were back on the rock.

"Wait here, please, bunny," said Elsby. "I'm going to get my stuff."

But the moment she turned, the rabbit bolted.

Elsby sighed. She was about to trudge back to the rock when she heard a branch crack behind her.

She whirled around and squinted into the dark forest. Maybe the rabbit was still there, watching her. Or maybe there was a deer. That would be interesting, too. She scanned the trees.

Or a bear—*were* there bears in Rhode Island?

She gasped.

It was not a rabbit, not a deer, not a bear.

A cat peered at her from the woods.

Not a normal cat. It stood on its two hind paws, and it was wearing *clothes*.

Olden-days clothes, too, like a poor little rich orphan from a storybook, or a Beatrix Potter tale: short blue pants, a white-and-blue sailor top, and a jaunty straw hat with two holes which his ears poked through. His fur was the dark gray of a summer storm cloud, and he had a broad, flat face and bright yellow eyes that gazed unblinking at Elsby. On his arm was a basket brimming with emerald-green . . .

Elsby squinted.

Was that really *broccoli?*

Wait. Maybe the cat was actually a statue.

Elsby stared, hardly daring to breathe.

The cat blinked.

"Hello," Elsby said, exhaling. "I—my name is Elsby—"

The cat turned and dashed—*on his two hind legs! Holding his basket!*—deeper into the dark woods.

"Wait! Please come back!" cried Elsby, plunging into the trees after him. Her own straw hat fell off, but she didn't stop to grab it. "Please!"

Thorns and vines scratched at her bare legs. Her sandal strap caught on a root and yanked at her ankle.

Hat ribbons rippling, the cat disappeared behind a ridge of bramble as Elsby watched, helpless to catch up.

She gripped a pine branch, trying to shake her foot free. When she looked up again, she wasn't sure in which direction the cat had gone. She took a few steps one way, then another, before she remembered about the ticks.

Elsby picked up her hat and backed out of the woods, her heart thrumming.

The cat in the woods was not like any cat Elsby had seen before. There was something almost *human* about the way it looked at her and the way it walked. And what kind of cat wore clothes, anyway? Not just a sweater, or booties, but an actual outfit. A shirt and pants. Buttons and ribbons. A *hat*!

Elsby rubbed pine resin off her fingers with a clump of damp moss. Then she hastened along the path to the rosebushes and the rock, where she gathered her notebook and pencils into her tote with trembling hands and hurried toward the front of the house.

When she reached the porch steps, she saw the cobwebbed door of Aunt Verity's dead landlady and shivered.

But she didn't notice the furry black face with glowing green eyes staring down at her from the window above.

CHAPTER THREE

The Cat Wearing Clothes

"I saw a cat!" said Elsby, bursting into Aunt Verity's warm kitchen.

The room looked like a valentine. It had red cabinets with curly white trim and a candy-red refrigerator with a rust-flecked silver handle. Her mother and great-aunt sat at a small, round table.

They both turned to look at her.

"A strange cat," said Elsby.

"I hope you didn't pet it," said her mother, and shuddered. She was so terribly allergic to cats she often said just thinking about one made her sneeze.

Aunt Verity raised one eyebrow and smiled slightly. "I've glimpsed a few cats around here myself. *Strange* cats."

Elsby peeked at Aunt Verity, who stared back at her

steadily, as if she was waiting for Elsby to continue.

"Would you like some tea, too, Elsby?" Aunt Verity asked. A plump yellow teapot with little matching yellow cups steamed beside Aunt Verity's elbow, like a mother hen and her brood of chicks.

"Okay," said Elsby. Dropping her hat and tote on the floor, she sank down in the seat beside Aunt Verity. "Tea is nice."

"Say *thank you*," whispered Elsby's mother.

"Thank you, Aunt Verity," said Elsby.

"Not to worry, dear," said Aunt Verity.

Elsby caught her breath as Aunt Verity poured the tea. Then she blurted out, "The cat was wearing clothes."

Elsby's mother looked at her. Wisps of her dark blond curls pressed against her sweaty forehead, and one side of her mouth curled in a half smile. "Clothes? Like a costume? A *cat?*"

"Olden-days clothes," said Elsby. She glanced at her great-aunt, who seemed intrigued. Elsby hurriedly looked away. "A sailor suit. Kind of like . . . you know, Beatrix Potter or something."

"A sailor suit!" exclaimed Elsby's mother. "I guess you have some eccentric neighbors, Verity. Dressing their cats!"

"Usually I think *I* am the eccentric neighbor," said Aunt Verity, smiling. "But it's true Snipatuit is an . . . unusual . . .

town. I've seen a few cats in strange garb around the neighborhood. Very puzzling."

"It was wearing a hat, too," said Elsby. She looked at her mother, but she was tapping away at her phone.

"Milk, Elsby?" offered Aunt Verity.

Elsby nodded, and Aunt Verity poured a splash from a small carton into Elsby's cup. Elsby hoped Aunt Verity didn't think she was lying.

"It was weird. I mean, cats don't wear clothes, or hats. Right?" said Elsby, watching the milk swirl into the tea like a billowing thundercloud.

"Dr. Seuss would beg to differ," said her mother, glancing up.

"You know that's not what I mean," said Elsby, frowning. "It walked on its hind legs," she added.

Her mother was still grinning, like she was searching for the next line of a joke. But Aunt Verity looked serious. Very serious. She stared at Elsby as though she was waiting for her to go on.

That was almost worse than being teased. Elsby clammed up.

"Sounds very charming. Promise me if you pet it, you'll wash your hands?" Elsby's mother shuddered again. "My eyes water just thinking about cats."

Eyes. That was it, Elsby realized. The cat's eyes were the weirdest of all.

"I'm not explaining right." Elsby took a deep breath. "It wasn't just the clothes and the way it walked. The cat—its eyes . . . It didn't seem like a *normal* cat."

"Was it foaming at the mouth?" Elsby's mother looked at Aunt Verity. "Is there a rabies problem up here?"

"Oh my goodness, no. Not as far as I'm aware." Aunt Verity pressed a hand to her chest.

"Not *rabies*, Mom." Elsby sighed, frustrated. "Not like it was sick. It was like . . . It was like it wanted to say something. I wish I could have taken a picture of the cat," Elsby said.

Elsby had a very basic cellphone—the flip-open kind with no camera or real Internet access. For a while she had also owned a cheap digital point-and-shoot camera, but it had broken quickly.

"I'm sorry, honey." Her mother looked guilty. "Do you have enough space in your notebook? I should have bought you a new one before we left the city."

One thing her mother was really good at was making sure Elsby had enough art supplies. Even when money was very tight, she did what she could to keep her in pencils and paper and paint, and tracked the sales at the art stores in New York. Good materials weren't cheap, but Elsby's mother felt they were important.

"Yes, thanks," said Elsby. She felt bad for even mentioning wanting to take pictures. "It's really okay."

"Your mother told me how talented you are at writing and drawing. A budding author-illustrator," said Aunt Verity.

Elsby gulped a big mouthful of tea, even though it was still hotter than she liked, just so she wouldn't have to respond. Then she said, "There was something even weirder about the cat. It was carrying—"

Ping. Ping. Ping.

"Oh, shoot!" Elsby's mother pulled out her phone again and jabbed at the screen until the blaring alert stopped. "I have to leave ASAP to meet Dirk at the airport with the car and catch my flight. So much driving!"

It was only after Elsby was outside, limply waving as her mother sputtered down Silver Crescent in Dirk's old car, that she remembered she had forgotten to finish sharing the oddest thing of all about the cat: its basket of broccoli.

Now that her mother was gone, Elsby felt shy—too shy to mention it to Aunt Verity, who stood beside her on the porch and was practically a stranger.

"Well, my dear. I'm looking forward to getting to know you." Aunt Verity clasped her hands together. "Dinner is at six. You have a few hours to play, or do whatever you'd like, or rest. Do you need anything? Please don't hesitate to ask."

Elsby tasted tears. It never got easier watching her

mother leave. She tried to stop the spiral of thinking about car accidents, or plane crashes, or a giant earthquake shaking LA to rubble while her mother was setting up the exhibition—and what would happen to Elsby then? She had no good answer to that question.

There was a truth Elsby avoided ever saying aloud. Unspoken, unacknowledged, it nevertheless was the foundation of every part of her being. In the entire world, there was only one person who truly loved her: her mother.

"You just let me know," Aunt Verity said, and gently patted her on the shoulder.

CHAPTER FOUR

A Tap at the Window

Elsby spent the afternoon wandering around the garden. The sky thickened and grayed, and the air cooled. A damp wind rushed through the trees and nudged the green leaves to show their silvery bellies. She sketched some roses, and then sat on a rock and tried to finish writing the first chapter of one of the novels she was working on.

This one was titled *Arabella of Manhattan*. It was about a girl who rescued animals from dreadful and perilous situations. In the opening scene, Arabella spotted a guinea pig dying of heatstroke in the backseat of a minivan near Central Park. Elsby needed to write the next scene, in which Arabella was arrested for breaking the car window to save it, but she was having trouble focusing.

She couldn't stop thinking about cats.

Elsby longed for her own pet. Not just a rodent or bird that lived in a cage. Something you could play with and cuddle.

A dog in their apartment was impossible. Their building didn't allow them, and her mother dared not "rock the boat," as she called it, by asking for an exception. She was always afraid the landlady would raise the rent.

A cat *was* allowed. Elsby's favorite thing—besides drawing and reading and writing—was borrowing her mother's laptop to look up homeless cats on animal shelter websites. She kept a list of favorites in her notebook and rejoiced, in a bittersweet way, when their profiles were updated to "*Adopted!*"

Elsby daydreamed about miracles like finding an abandoned kitten meowing from a garbage can on her walk to school and being allowed to keep it.

Except.

Elsby's mother was allergic to cats. Not just a little bit. Like, *really* allergic—the coughing, wheezing, hives-everywhere kind of allergic.

Putting down her pencil, she stood up and began pacing the garden. She wanted to find the strange gray cat in clothes again.

She studied the neighbors' yards, but they were as silent and cat-less as her own.

The wind picked up and carried the scent of rain.

"Dinnertime, Elsby!" Aunt Verity called from the kitchen window, and Elsby hurried inside.

While her great aunt finished setting the table, Elsby looked around the living room. It was cluttered with cuckoo clocks, books, old photographs in wooden frames, and baskets of half-finished quilting projects. It was cozily chaotic, like a nice thrift store.

"It's ready," said Aunt Verity, popping her head through the doorway.

In the kitchen, two plates of grilled cheese sandwiches and frilly green salads sat on the table. A box fan hummed in the window, blowing damp summery air into the room and making the curtain dance. Outside, above the wall of green-black trees at the end of the garden, the magenta sky was streaked with orange.

"Thank you," said Elsby, sinking down into the chair her great-aunt gestured toward.

"Your mother said grilled cheese was one of your favorite foods," said Aunt Verity, leaning over to switch on a lamp. "I love mine with bacon."

Elsby picked up the sandwich and took a quick bite. It was salty, crunchy, and delicious.

"One of the benefits of my line of work is that I get summers off," said Aunt Verity. "So I will be around most of the day while you're here. Though I do still need time to read, and write, and prepare my lectures, and I also volunteer delivering meals to the elderly. But I'm hoping we'll have some fun while you visit. This weekend I'll take you to a special place in town, the Snipatuit Athenaeum." Aunt Verity picked up her knife and fork and carefully cut her sandwich into pieces.

"The what?"

"Ah-tha-NEE-um. It's an old-fashioned term for a kind of private library. We have one here in Snipatuit that looks like a castle. I'm a member."

"You have to pay?" Elsby frowned and stabbed at her salad.

Aunt Verity swallowed the forkful of sandwich she'd just eaten, and then spoke. "It's not so terribly expensive to join, and they do have free events sometimes. There's a town library here, too. The Athenaeum is just a little different."

Elsby finished her sandwich and started on the salad. Her mother favored vinegar salad dressings, but whatever Aunt Verity had put on this one was sugary-sweet. It was like a lettuce dessert.

"There is the outdoors to explore, too, of course. There's a park near the town square, and some coffee shops and such." Aunt Verity hesitated, as though she wasn't quite sure of what she was about to say. "Your mother said it was all right for you to walk around town by yourself, so long as you have your phone turned on."

"Yeah. I walk home alone from school all the time," Elsby said.

Aunt Verity nodded. "Well, you're welcome to stick close to the house, too. The garden out back is a bit disheveled, unfortunately—it was my landlady's, and I haven't been able to keep up with the weeding since she passed on."

The wind gusted, teetering the box fan and billowing the curtains.

"We may get thunderstorms tonight," said Aunt Verity, leaning over to push the fan back into place. "I'll give you a flashlight. Sometimes the power goes out around here."

Thunderstorms! Elsby loved weather and storms and even power outages. They were exciting.

She looked around the kitchen as she slowly chewed up the last wisps of frisée lettuce. "I like the way your kitchen is decorated," she said. "The whole house, really."

"I wish I could take credit for it, but I rented this place furnished. My dear old landlady, Rose, was an antiques collector. She had a fine eye."

"I like the outside of the house, too. It feels kind of like . . . like a fairy tale." Elsby pinched a stray lettuce leaf from her fork and stuck it in her mouth.

"Doesn't it?" Aunt Verity smiled, her eyes twinkling. "The style is called Carpenter Gothic. It was popular in the late eighteen hundreds."

"I wish houses were still made this way. Like fairy tales. I don't understand why they can't be."

Elsby expected to get a lecture about modernity, and change, and the need for eco-friendly building materials. Things her mother liked to talk about.

But Aunt Verity's smile changed to something a bit more melancholy. "You and me both," she said with a sigh.

The first peals of thunder arrived as Elsby lay in the narrow bed in her temporary room, sketching in her notebook by the light of the flashlight. It was dark outside. The power had not gone out, but she liked the flashlight anyway; it felt atmospheric.

The room was in the attic, and its ceiling slanted down on one side. There was a single window that looked out on a thin, flat part of the roof at the front of the house. A flaking white wooden railing marched around the roof's edge. It was *almost* like a balcony, something that Elsby had always wanted back in Brooklyn.

The thought of home pinched Elsby's heart like it was a piece of Play-Doh. She'd packed up her most precious things—her sketchbooks, best stuffed animals, baby photo albums—and shoved them in the closet her mother promised would stay locked while they were gone. But what if the strangers were going through the rest of their stuff? Experimenting with her art supplies? Rearranging her books? Using—and maybe breaking—her favorite mug with the skiing penguin on the side?

She gritted her teeth thinking about it, then swung the flashlight around.

Her great-aunt's spare room was a kind of museum. Not an art museum like the ones her mother worked for, but a history museum cluttered with curious things from the past. The bed was small and wooden, with a patchwork quilt of pink-, red-, and cream-colored diamonds. An old metal sewing machine hunched in one corner below a shelf of porcelain dolls with matted hair and eyes that gleamed in the beam of light. Elsby quickly looked away from them.

More thunder rumbled. The wind gusted against the house and swirled through the screen of the half-open window. Elsby remembered Aunt Verity's dead land-lady—was her name Rose?—and turned on the tiny table lamp. Then she opened her notebook again.

Her drawing of the mysterious cat peered up at her. She had managed to get down most of what she could remember about his outfit, and even included the broccoli in the basket. In her best cursive—she and her friend Helen were the only two who kept practicing the fancy handwriting after the unit ended—she had written:

Rhode Island. THE CAT.

Elsby shut her notebook, switched off the lamp again, and leaned back on the thin pillow. She tried to imagine who lived in this room in the olden days. Maybe a maid. An orphaned maid. *Semi*-orphaned, because her father never cared about her, and her mother had to travel to faraway lands to earn money for their daily gruel. The maid had been sent to the countryside to work in the house of a distant relation. . . .

It wasn't a bad idea, and Elsby was always looking for new ideas. Good ones. She had begun over a dozen novels but never gotten further than writing the first chapter of any of them.

She sat up, clicked the lamp on, and opened her notebook again. She began scribbling an outline of the story. She decided the tragic maid should be called Harriet Millicent Montgomery. Picking names—for people, and pets, and towns and streets—was the easiest part of writing.

"Hmm . . . or maybe Dorothy," she murmured, tapping the pencil on her lip. "Dorothy Francesca Hollandaise . . . She could live in a village called . . . Amethyst Hollow.

On a street called Emerald Crescent. Yes . . . And she's very lonely."

Elsby was tempted to grab her thesaurus from her suitcase and look up synonyms for *lonely*. It was one of the things she did when she wasn't sure what to write next.

Tap.

Elsby stiffened.

Tap tap tap.

The window. Something was knocking on it. A twig? No.

It sounded like a . . . fingernail.

Elsby thought again of that dead landlady. Rose.

Did ghosts have fingernails?

Heart pounding, Elsby slowly turned around.

Not a fingernail.

A *claw.*

Three furry faces and several pink paws were pressed against the window. One face belonged to the same dark gray cat she had seen in the woods. He was still wearing his sailor suit, though he had taken off his little straw hat. The two others wore lacy bonnets, like old-fashioned ladies.

Except they weren't ladies.

They were *cats*!

One was cream-colored, with longish hair and amber eyes, and the other was black as a clear night sky, with brightly glinting green eyes. The eyes of the cat in the sailor suit were a vivid copper.

Elsby tiptoed toward the window. The cats gazed at her steadily. They leaned back when she began to open the window and the screen.

"Hello," said Elsby, trying to stay calm.

The three cats looked at one another. Then the one in the sailor suit stepped forward.

"We need to speak to you," he said.

CHAPTER FIVE

Marzipan, Tapioca, Horatio, and Clarissa

Elsby blinked at the cats. She opened her mouth, but no words came out.

"Fiddlesticks! Does it even know how to talk?" hissed the pale, fluffy one, who wore a frilly, snow-colored dress with an eyelet-lace pinafore and matching bonnet. She wrinkled her nose. "Little humans only cry and speak gibberish at first. Perhaps it's too small to help us. I knew this was a bad plan."

"Hush, Clarissa," whispered the black cat, who wore a royal purple dress with black lace trim and a black apron. "The child is simply in shock. Remember, humans talk to cats all the time, but they never expect us to answer back."

She turned to Elsby and smiled. *Did* cats smile?

"I'm Marzipan Fairweather," continued the black cat.

"And you're Elsby, is that right?"

"Uh . . . yes. Short for Elisabeth with an *s*," said Elsby, gripping the windowsill. "I'm Elisabeth MacBride."

Her thoughts were racing. What was happening? Was she dreaming? Were these cats—these cats wearing clothes!—really *speaking* to her?

"I'm Horatio Fairweather," said the cat in the sailor suit. "It's a pleasure to meet you."

"Clarissa," said the white cat, frowning.

Could cats frown?

"I apologize for the surprise," said Marzipan, adjusting her bonnet. "We need you to come with us to our house. It's just next-door. Can you manage the roof? It's a few paces to the other window."

"Don't be silly, Marzipan," said Clarissa. "She'll fall! Just think how the humans build their houses! Stairs with silly banisters and tiny steps and carpeting so they don't plummet to their deaths every time they try to climb higher than a sofa."

"Am I dreaming?" Elsby whispered, slowly exhaling.

"No. You are awake," said Horatio.

"Very awake. See?" Clarissa reached across the windowsill to press a claws-out paw against Elsby's hand.

"Ouch!" Elsby cried.

"Clarissa!" Marzipan hissed.

Clarissa shrugged. "Now she knows she's not dreaming."

"Clarissa was simply helping her, Marzipan," said Horatio.

Marzipan rolled her eyes.

"Do—do all the animals in this town talk?" Elsby was thinking of the rabbits.

"No, only us," said Marzipan.

"We're quite rare," said Clarissa.

"So, can you manage the roof? I hope you can. It's that, or the front door," said Horatio. "Could you sneak down the stairs past your aunt's room?"

"*Humans* and *sneak* don't belong in the same sentence," muttered Clarissa. "I swear their paws—excuse me, feet—are made of rocks."

Elsby picked up her flashlight, stuck her head out the window, and swung the beam over the roof. Thunder pealed. It was getting closer. Clouds scuttled across the moon. It would rain soon.

"Roof," Elsby said. "I'll be fine."

"Follow us," said Horatio.

"And if you start to fall, don't pull our tails," said Clarissa, arching an eyebrow at Elsby. Cats, it turned out, also had eyebrows, or at least the suggestion of them.

"I would never do that!" said Elsby, heat rising to her cheeks.

"Don't be so hard on her, Clarissa," said Marzipan. "Remember, we need her help."

Help.

"I want to help," Elsby hurried to say. "I always want to help animals. What—"

"Lose the flashlight," said Clarissa. "Someone could see it."

Elsby put her flashlight back on the side table. Then she hesitated. She wasn't supposed to go anywhere with strangers. These were cats, but still . . .

"Maybe I should get my great-aunt. I'm sure she would be happy to try to help—"

"No adults!" the three cats hissed in unison.

"Adults would split us up and send us off to the pound!" said Clarissa.

"Or worse," said Marzipan in a low voice. "And you, Clarissa, certainly can't be trusted not to *talk* in front of them."

"The incident with the plumber was many years ago," said Clarissa. "We agreed not to discuss it anymore."

"I promise we won't harm you, Elsby," said Marzipan. "We are taking a risk, too, speaking with you. No one else knows our secret."

"All right," said Elsby.

She turned back to the bedroom and grabbed her pencil. They were only cats, after all. Talking cats— *talking cats!*—but cats, nonetheless. How dangerous could they be?

Elsby dashed out a note on a scrap of paper:

Aunt Verity—I went to your old landlady's side of the house to check on some cats I saw. Back soon. Elsby.

She left it on her pillow.

"This way," whispered Horatio when Elsby had climbed out through the window onto the roof.

"Don't touch the trimming, kid," said Clarissa. "Unless you want to die."

Elsby yanked her hand back from the white railing.

"It's unstable," said Marzipan in a gentler tone.

Putting one foot carefully in front of the other, Elsby followed Horatio and Marzipan. The roof ledge was narrow, but perfectly flat. The two cats stopped at the next window. It was wide-open.

Horatio hopped inside, followed by Marzipan.

"Move it," snapped Clarissa, who was behind her.

Elsby swung her legs through the open window. Clarissa slithered in after her. Marzipan turned and shut the window.

"I can hardly see," said Elsby.

"I will never understand how you humans evolved to run the world, despite your myriad weaknesses," said Clarissa. "Imagine not being able to see in the dark!"

Elsby's eyes, adjusting to the dimness, made out the

shadows of four small, canopied beds the right size for dolls—or cats.

"Hold my paw, Elsby," said Marzipan. "I won't scratch you, I promise. There are two flights of steps. Downstairs are both shades and heavy curtains, so we can turn on some lights. I forgot how delicate human eyes are."

Marzipan's paw was fuzzy and warm, and Elsby relaxed.

"Hold the railing as we go. My sister is waiting for us," said Marzipan. Louder, she called, "Tappy! Turn on the lamp. The human is here."

A light switched on, and Elsby saw the narrow staircase led to an entry hall and a front door, the perfect mirror of her great aunt's home. There was old-fashioned striped wallpaper, like a pink candy cane, and many round and square framed pictures on the walls.

A black cat with white paws and ears, wearing a blue calico dress with a white pinafore, peered around the doorway from the living room. She had watery blue eyes and a tiny pink nose.

"That is my sister, Tapioca Fairweather. Tappy for short. She was too scared to come with us to fetch you. Tappy, this is the human," said Marzipan as she nudged Elsby down the last few steps. "Her name is Elsby. She says she will help us."

"I mean, I *want* to help you, but I don't even

understand what kind of help you—"

"We'll discuss the particulars . . . shortly." Clarissa leaped down from the second floor and landed atop a bookshelf on the other side of the staircase, startling Elsby. "Get her tea and whatever else, Horatio. And hurry. We've wasted enough time already this evening. I need to get back to my studies."

What studies? Elsby wondered.

"Of course, Clarissa, of course," said Horatio, pattering smoothly down the stairs. "Do you like tea, Elsby? We have mint, or Earl Grey, or chai."

"Rose loved tea so much," whispered the black-and-white cat with a sniffle.

Marzipan hurried toward her sister, who began to weep.

"There, there, Tappy," whispered Marzipan, dabbing Tappy's cheeks with a handkerchief. "It's all right. Shh."

"I, um, don't need any tea, thank you," whispered Elsby.

She stepped awkwardly into what the cats called the parlor. It was not very different from Aunt Verity's living room, with a small sofa and two scratched-up looking armchairs, and more photographs and paintings on the walls.

"Biscuits, Elsby?" said Horatio. "We have some plain vanilla biscuits left behind when . . ."

Tappy's quiet tears turned to wailing. "R-r-rose loved biscuits!"

"Tapioca loves to mope," said Clarissa.

"She is *grieving*. Tappy is very sensitive," Marzipan shot back.

"Uh, it's okay, no biscuits either, thanks," said Elsby.

Tappy lowered the handkerchief and gazed directly at Elsby. "She's just so—so human! Just like Rose."

Marzipan dabbed her cheeks with the back of her paw, and Horatio delicately blew his nose. Clarissa rolled her eyes.

"Pull yourself together, Horatio," Clarissa hissed. "I expect waterworks from those two sad sacks, but not you. Tears! From *cats*! Disgusting!"

"You're right, Clarissa, you're right. So sorry," said Horatio, stuffing his handkerchief into his pocket. "Well, let's all gather round and make our appeal to the child. Come along, everyone. Elsby, please sit."

He gestured to the sofa, and Elsby perched on the edge of one of the cushions.

"Welcome to Snipatuit," said Clarissa.

"I'm really sorry for your loss, all of you." Elsby looked from cat to cat. "It sounds like you really loved Rose."

"She is—was—wonderful. The best human ever." Tappy looked up at Elsby with red-rimmed eyes. "Do you want to see our shrine to her?"

Thunder boomed, followed by a flash of lightning. Elsby jumped.

The cats stared at her.

"Uh, sure," Elsby said. It seemed rude to decline, and besides, she was curious.

The cats led her to what should have been the kitchen pantry. A few cans of tuna were scattered across otherwise bare shelves. On a small upside-down cardboard box covered in a red cloth was a collection of candles, dried and fresh flowers in vases, and a box of tea. At the center was a framed photograph of a beautiful older woman with long, silvery gray hair, light skin, and a kind smile. She looked like the kind of person who would make pottery and go on long backpacking adventures in remote forests.

"Our dear Rose," murmured Marzipan.

All the cats—even Clarissa—bowed their heads and shut their eyes. Elsby hastily did the same, keeping one eye cracked until the cats looked up again.

"May she rest in peace," said Horatio.

"I miss her so much," whimpered Tappy. "I was so sure she would have shown herself by now. Come back to see us . . ."

"Come back to see you?" Elsby's skin prickled. "What do you mean?"

"Cats have a knack for seeing ghosts, you know," said

Marzipan. "We've never had much trouble spotting them."

Elsby glanced at the room, hugging her own arms.

"There was the handyman from nineteen-oh-two. He didn't realize he'd fallen off the roof and died," said Horatio. "So he just kept inspecting the house's drainpipes."

"For over a hundred years," said Marzipan.

"So tedious," said Clarissa.

"And the little boy who succumbed to the great Providence cholera epidemic of eighteen fifty-four. Poor mite," said Marzipan.

"But don't fret," said Horatio, smiling gently at Elsby. "Our Rose was a skilled healer, and she helped all of them pass on to the other side in peace. No ghosts linger here."

"She was the best human there ever was," whispered Tappy.

"Also the only human we actually knew," said Clarissa. "And who knew about us."

"We are in dire straits without her," said Marzipan. "That's why we need your help, Elsby. Let's go back to the parlor, and we will explain more to you about our predicament."

Elsby sat down on the sofa again, glancing around warily. Marzipan perched on her left, sitting upright like a human, with her sister Tappy curled in a ball beside her.

Horatio sat on Elsby's right. Clarissa lay on the rug with her chin resting on one snow-white paw. She smoothed her lacy dress with the other.

"Rose passed on very suddenly." Marzipan folded her paws primly on her lap and stared at Elsby, her shoulders stiff. "She just managed to call nine-one-one and tell us to hide before she staggered out to the porch and . . ."

Marzipan trailed off, and Tappy let out a wail.

"She always kept some emergency provisions for us, but now we're running low," said Marzipan, patting her sister's shoulder. "We've been reduced to borrowing from our neighbors' gardens when they are at work."

Elsby raised her eyebrows, thinking about the broccoli.

"To be fair, humans just *leave* it all out there," said Clarissa. "Anyone could come and borrow it. Tomatoes, watermelon . . . broccoli."

"You can't borrow food, exactly," murmured Elsby. "I mean, not after you eat it."

"You're right of course. It's thievery, and it's shameful. But we're desperate. We don't plan to continue imposing on our neighbors in such a way," said Marzipan.

"Besides, we loathe broccoli," said Horatio, and shuddered.

"Why not catch some . . . I don't know . . . mice?" asked Elsby.

Four pairs of eyes gazed at her in silent horror.

"I'm sorry," said Elsby, though she didn't quite know what she was apologizing for.

Horatio took a dramatic breath like he was recovering from a bout of nausea. "We are not the type of cats who eat mice—not since we . . ."

The cats exchanged nervous glances.

". . . changed," said Marzipan, not meeting Elsby's eyes.

"We prefer chicken, tuna, flounder. All cooked, of course," said Horatio.

"Though we did enjoy the sashimi that Rose ordered in for us every Christmas, as a treat," said Marzipan.

"We even like the wasabi," said Horatio. "It was so exciting when the first Japanese restaurant opened around here back in the nineteen eighties."

Elsby squinted at him. "Excuse me. Did you say 'the nineteen eighties'?"

"Perhaps I didn't," said Horatio, after a pause.

"But—that would make you—" Elsby tried to do the math. No way. Cats couldn't live that long.

But then again, cats weren't supposed to talk, either.

"How old are you?" asked Elsby. She stared at each cat in turn, but each looked away.

"Haven't you heard it's rude to ask someone's age?" said Clarissa, examining her claws. "Tsk-tsk."

More thunder rumbled, and the lamp flickered.

"Oh. Sorry." Elsby turned toward Marzipan. "It's just . . .

You can talk *and* you are older than any other cats in the history of cats. Can someone *please* explain?"

"All in due time," said Marzipan. "First, we need your help. Rose always told us that if we were ever in desperate need, to ask a child."

"So we sent Horatio out to observe you this afternoon," said Clarissa.

"It's always *me* who gets forced into these things," muttered Horatio.

"I know. I saw you in the woods," said Elsby.

"Horatio!" hissed Clarissa. "You doofus. You were supposed to be discreet!"

"You *never* should have worn clothes, Horatio. That's how we'll get discovered," said Marzipan.

"I loathe being naked," said Horatio, and rolled his eyes to the ceiling.

"We all do," said Clarissa. "Could anything be more mortifying? Well, maybe a fear of heights, like humans and rabbits have. Silly creatures."

"I'm not really afraid of heights," said Elsby, but none of the cats seemed to hear her.

"I knew I should have been the one to go," said Marzipan. "I have more grit in these situations."

"Anyway, no harm done," said Horatio, coughing into the handkerchief he pulled from his pocket again. "To return to our topic, Rose always said a child would be more likely to believe us and less likely to betray us."

"I won't betray you," said Elsby. "But I need to know what you want."

"You must promise not to tell that human you are living with about us," said Marzipan.

"My great-aunt Verity? But she wouldn't hurt you. She's really nice."

"That's what they all say," hissed Clarissa. "But humans cannot be trusted, ever. When no one adopts you from the shelter after ninety days, they put you down."

"As if you and Horatio were ever really at risk of *that*, Clarissa," said Marzipan.

Clarissa glowered at her. "You, of all cats, should know better than to put your faith in humans, Marzipan."

"Rose adopted Horatio and Clarissa from a rich old lady who often visited the library where Rose worked," said Marzipan, turning to Elsby. "When those two lived with their first owner, before she went to a nursing home, they ate caviar practically every day. They're purebred after all—Clarissa is a Persian cat and Horatio is a British Shorthair."

"Clarissa's mother was a beauty queen," said Horatio, giving her an admiring glance. "She won lots of award ribbons at shows."

"And she deserved each one," said Clarissa.

"No doubt," said Marzipan. "But admit it. You and

Horatio have never known true suffering."

Clarissa made a small *hrmph*.

"Um . . . how did you and Tappy end up with Rose, Marzipan?" Elsby asked.

Fresh tears rolled down Tappy's cheeks.

"I mean, if it's not too traumatic to talk about," Elsby hurried to add.

"We were born as strays on the mean streets of downtown Providence, Rhode Island," Marzipan said after a long pause. "Many hungry days and cold nights marked our kittenhood. We lived under a bridge covered in icicles and ate garbage people threw into the gutters."

"Pitiful," said Horatio.

"We were picked up by animal control, and then abandoned at a shelter, where Rose saw us shivering together. She adopted us on the spot. Otherwise we would never have made it," said Marzipan.

"The humans running the place had marked them for death if they weren't adopted that very evening," said Clarissa. "Breathtaking cruelty."

"I'm so sorry you went through that," murmured Elsby.

"Rose was our guardian angel," said Marzipan.

"I will never go back to a shelter. Never, never, never," wept Tappy.

Elsby fell silent for a moment. "Okay. I promise not to mention you all to Aunt Verity. But I can't agree to help you without knowing what you need," she said.

"We need you to get us groceries," said Marzipan. "And quickly."

Elsby's eyes widened. "Wait. If you're asking me to *steal*—"

"We would never!" cried Horatio. "We have more honor than that."

"Careful, Horatio. We aren't *dogs*," said Clarissa.

"We have money, Elsby, and we would never ask you to break the law. In addition to groceries, we're also hoping you can . . ."

Marzipan paused, and all of the cats exchanged glances.

"Not yet, Marzipan," Clarissa murmured in a voice so quiet Elsby almost missed her words.

Marzipan took a deep breath. "We're also hoping you can bring us . . . new reading material!" Her round little face broke into a broad, toothy smile. Her eyes sparkled like green traffic lights.

"I would love to help you, but . . . how? I don't even know where the grocery store is. If I go food shopping with my aunt, she'll ask questions when I try to buy a bag of kibble or whatever."

"We do not eat kibble!" the cats shouted in unison.

"Okay! Yikes!" Elsby threw her hands up.

"It will be easy. Your aunt is often out of the house," said Marzipan.

"The grocery store is just a few streets away," said Horatio. "One of us will pretend to be a regular, naked cat—"

They all winced.

"—and guide you there. We'll give you cash."

"Our dear Rose provided for us so well," sniffled Tappy.

"Tomorrow," said Marzipan. "As soon as your aunt leaves. Agreed?"

"I guess so," said Elsby. "I just—I just don't understand. *How* can you speak? And how are you so old? I don't mean to be rude, it's just—it's not exactly natural."

"In good time we'll tell you everything," said Horatio. "For now, all we need is your help getting food."

"And books. That's it," said Marzipan.

"For now," Clarissa said. She stretched out her claws and peered down at them. Elsby noticed they were very sharp and painted bright blood red.

CHAPTER SIX

Vanilla Pudding and Ten Pounds of Liver

Early the next morning, Elsby sat in bed, staring down at her hands. They were streaked with dirt. It was grime from the roof. She stared at the open window of her attic room. The screen hung slightly askew.

Elsby's heart pounded. None of it had been a dream.

The cats were real.

"Elsby! Your mother is on the phone!" Aunt Verity's voice rose, muffled, from somewhere downstairs.

Elsby shoved her hands back under the covers. "I'm here!" she called.

Her great-aunt knocked twice on Elsby's door and then gently opened it. With a hesitant smile on her face, she held out a big clunky phone with an antenna. A landline! Elsby shot one hand out and grabbed it.

"Breakfast is ready, too. I need to head out soon for a few errands." Aunt Verity waved and shut the door behind her.

Elsby put the phone to her ear.

"Sweetie, I just landed and I'm walking to my bag. All's fine. How are you settling—"

Elsby's mother's voice was interrupted by the blaring garble of an airport loudspeaker.

"Fine," Elsby said when it was quiet again. The phone felt like a huge plastic pillow tucked against her shoulder.

"Heading to the hotel now—I *think* I'm at the right door. Hold on, that's my driver—or is it? I gotta go in a minute, Gumdrop. But how are you?"

Elsby swung her legs over the side of the bed. She tried to think of everything she wanted to tell her mother, starting with the cats. But how?

"Elsby?"

"I'm so glad your plane didn't crash," she blurted out.

"Elsby . . . we've talked about this. Statistically . . ."

Tears of relief blurred Elsby's eyes as her mother started to lecture about how flying was safer than driving.

"Anyway, I have to hit the ground running here, write some emails and all that boring stuff. Sweetie, be good for Aunt Verity, okay? I know you will be. Call me if you have any problems, all right? Let's talk again before bed. I love you."

Elsby wiped her eyes. "I love you, Mom."

It wasn't until she heard the phone drone—landlines were so strange—that Elsby realized she had entirely forgotten to mention the cats.

There was a tiny bathroom across the attic hallway. Elsby scrubbed her hands clean in the chipped sink, brushed her teeth, and stared into the scratched mirror. She shook loose her hair, combed out her bangs, and wove her hair into two thick braids that hung below her shoulders. Then she washed her glasses in the sink, dried them on the edge of her nightgown, and pushed them back onto her face, sighing with relief. She didn't feel fully herself without them.

Back in her room, she pulled on the long blue dress with the lace collar she'd gotten from the Halloween section of the Salvation Army on Broadway. She grabbed her tote bag, cellphone, notebook, and pencils, and headed downstairs, stashing the landline phone under her arm to return to Aunt Verity.

Breakfast was waffles from a real iron press, with strawberries, whipped cream, and freshly squeezed orange juice.

It was clear Aunt Verity had made an effort, and when she offered to bring Elsby along on her morning errands, Elsby felt bad saying no.

"All right. Well, keep your cell on." Aunt Verity

shuffled through a cupboard by the door. "Here's the house key."

Elsby stood on the porch and waved as her great-aunt pulled out of the driveway in her silver station wagon.

A curtain of gauzy clouds hid the sun, but the air was thick and already hot.

From the corner of her eye, she saw a fuzzy black cat—with no clothes—standing beside a tree, staring at her with eyes that glowed like two green lollipops.

"Marzipan?" Elsby whispered.

The cat dashed over on all four legs and pattered up the porch steps. A tiny purple velvet pouch dangled from a string around her neck.

"Good morning," said the cat.

"Hello, Marzipan," said Elsby, crouching down. "I almost didn't recognize you."

"Don't remind me." Marzipan shuddered. "What they say is true—the clothes make the cat. I feel so naked!"

"Well, I think you look perfectly normal."

"Right. That says more about you than me. Untie the pouch," said Marzipan, gesturing at it with her chin. "It has the money and the grocery list. Put it in your pocket until we get to the store. Follow me but don't act like you know me. Watch for cars—they're beastly."

"I despise cars," said Elsby.

"Sensible of you," said Marzipan. "Clarissa would be impressed."

Elsby followed Marzipan down Silver Crescent. Cicadas hummed in the trees along the street, but otherwise it was very quiet. Even on the main road there was almost no traffic. Marzipan turned left and kept close to the lawns, darting from bush to scraggly bush and waiting in clumps of flowers for Elsby to catch up.

Snipatuit was sleepy. Many of its houses were squat, slightly crooked Colonial-era cottages with pitched roofs and tiny windows. Elsby expected the Puritans from her social studies book to come stalking through the low doorways in their black hats. Other houses were more modern. Some driveways had boats parked in them. No people were out.

Marzipan turned left again, and they were on a busy road. They passed a sunbaked gas station that smelled like oil, and a Dunkin' Donuts with a busy parking lot, and then a strip of businesses. There was an antique shop, a nail salon, and best of all—a bookstore!

"Many Moons Books & Things—Used & New" was painted in silvery-white letters on a black, crescent-shaped sign that hung above the door. The store was closed, but Elsby pressed her face to the glass. She loved bookstores.

"I've heard it's a good one," Marzipan said, twisting

around Elsby's ankles. "I long to browse the shelves myself."

Then Marzipan ran ahead like a rippling shadow and Elsby had to race to catch up.

They reached a weed-choked brick square. Lording over it was an iron statue of a man with bushy eyebrows and a severe, eagle-like beak of a nose. He wore a hooded cape and stared down fiercely at a crystal ball he gripped in his hands.

"Algernon Endicott," whispered Marzipan. "A hundred years ago he pretty much owned this town."

Elsby was about to turn away when she noticed a strange word in capital letters carved at his feet:

REDIBO

"*Redibo?* What does that mean?" Elsby asked, looking down at Marzipan.

"You don't know Latin? Pitiful," said Marzipan. "It means 'I will return.'"

A chill raced down Elsby's spine, despite the summer heat. Return from . . . where?

"Let's keep going," said Marzipan, and Elsby was glad when they were beyond the statue's creepy gaze.

They passed two churches, and then a cemetery appeared. It was bordered by a mossy old stone wall.

"Almost there," Marzipan whispered. "It's right on the other side of that parking lot. I'll wait here. No one bothers a black cat in a burial ground."

The grocery store was called Roy's Farm & Food Mart. Elsby wondered what the "farm" part meant. She hoped there were live chickens or cows or something.

No such luck.

Inside it just looked like a normal grocery store, not so different from the cramped and cluttered ones back in New York. Fluorescent lights glowed on rows of packaged food. The air was cold and smelled damp.

Elsby dug the pouch out of her dress pocket and slowly opened it. Inside was a wad of cash and a small piece of paper covered in a delicate, spiderweb cursive. Cat handwriting—or paw writing, Elsby thought, to be more precise.

10 lbs. liver
10 lbs. fish (most economical variety)
10 lbs. chicken
4 gallons milk (full fat)
6 boxes vanilla pudding

"How am I going to carry all this?" Elsby murmured.

"Can I help you, miss?"

She looked up to find a wire-thin old man with tiny glasses staring down at her. He was snipping piles of flowers and arranging them in buckets by the doorway. She wondered if he was Roy.

"Er, um, sure. Can you point me to where the meat is?" she asked.

"The butcher is at the back," the man said, gesturing with his thumb.

"Thank you," said Elsby.

When she reached the counter, she heard footsteps behind her and turned.

It was the thin, elderly florist. "I'm also the butcher," he said, and stepped behind the display case. "Flowers, meat—I chop it all."

"Okay," said Elsby, nudging her glasses up her nose. She'd hoped the meat would be shrink-wrapped and sitting on trays so she wouldn't have to talk to anyone.

"What would you like, dear?"

"Um . . ." Elsby looked down at her list. "Well, do you have ten pounds of liver?"

"A tenth of a pound? You having a dinner party for some mice?" The man jutted out his bottom lip and squinted one eye, like he was thinking. "Well, I can try to get it that small, let's see." He turned and ripped a piece of paper from a roll.

"No, no. Wait," Elsby said. "Ten . . . *pounds.*"

The man looked back at her, cocking his head. "Ten *pounds?*"

Elsby stared at the wall behind him, not making eye contact. Long ago she had learned this was the best way to deal with curious strangers. "Yes. Ten pounds," she said, as if it was a most unremarkable amount to buy.

He frowned and pulled his chin into his neck in disbelief. "Whatcha cooking with that much liver?"

"Dinner."

Elsby had heard people in New England were famous for being reserved. The opposite of nosy. Rhode Island was part of New England. Now she hoped the man was a true New Englander and wouldn't ask any other questions.

"Well, I guess it'll be a nutritious one," he said, laying the paper down on the scale. "I think I have at least eight pounds. Sound good?"

Elsby nodded, relieved.

Elsby emerged from the grocery store sagging under the weight of several plastic bags. The sun had burned through the clouds. Elsby squinted. She had forgotten her hat. The grocery store parking lot was getting busier, and she had to avoid a few cars pulling into empty spaces as she maneuvered toward the graveyard.

Marzipan jumped from behind a tombstone near the wall. Without a word, she darted to the sidewalk. Then she began trotting back the way they had come.

Elsby struggled to keep up. Cars whizzed past,

hissing like huge beetles. She worried that Aunt Verity's was one of them. What would she say if she saw sweaty Elsby trudging down the sidewalk carrying all this stuff?

At last she reached cool and shady Silver Crescent. Marzipan sat primly in a beam of sunlight in front of Aunt Verity's house.

"Stash the bags behind the lilac bush," Marzipan said. "We'll carry them through a window later. Oh, and drop in the leftover money, if you don't mind."

Elsby looked around the yard, trying to figure out which plant was a lilac.

"That shaggy green one," said Marzipan, and tipped her chin toward a full, tall bush near the house. "Lilacs are quintessentially New England. Don't you know the Emily Dickinson poem 'It will be summer—eventually'?"

"Um, maybe?"

"Then you surely don't. Because it's *unforgettable.*"

Marzipan cleared her throat, then began to recite:

"The Lilacs—bending many a year—
Will sway with purple load—
The Bees—will not despise the tune—
Their Forefathers—have hummed—"

"That's really . . . mysterious. And nice," said Elsby.

"Emily Dickinson was a genius," said Marzipan as she scurried toward the bush. "Anyway, you should be able to identify a lilac, even without the flowers. It's essential knowledge."

"I would love to be able to know lilacs, but I don't even have a yard back home."

"Pitiful! A cooped-up house human is worse than a house cat. Well, it's this one here. Come."

The lilac was big enough to be a pretend cottage, and Elsby remembered when she was little and played in the bushes in Prospect Park—after her mother checked them for litter.

She put down the heavy bags with relief.

"Thank you," said Marzipan. "Just in time, too."

Elsby heard the sound of a car behind her and turned to see her great-aunt's small station wagon crunching up the gravel drive.

"Hello! Glad to see you out getting some fresh air," said Aunt Verity, closing the car door with a smile. "I went to the farmer's market."

Elsby glanced at the lilac, where the bags from the grocery store were just barely visible under the green froth of leaves. Marzipan had vanished.

"Let me help you," Elsby said, running up to Aunt Verity.

"Thank you," said Aunt Verity, handing over two tote bags. "I also stopped by the grocery store for some extra things your mom said you liked."

Elsby saw a receipt peeking out from one of the bags. Aunt Verity had gone to Roy's, too!

"We can go again in a few days to pick up anything I missed. Let's get this stuff in the house!"

Elsby helped put away the groceries, grateful that somehow she and Aunt Verity had not crossed paths at Roy's Farm & Food Mart. There were salad greens, deli cold cuts, green beans, peanut butter, and many other things.

"Oh, rats. I left some important stuff in the car," said Aunt Verity.

A few minutes later she was back.

"I just saw the strangest thing," Aunt Verity muttered, putting down two tote bags full of papers and books. "A *cat*, a black cat, dashing out of the lilac holding a plastic sack in its mouth."

Elsby looked up from the cupboard where she was stacking cans of chickpeas.

"Wow," she said, hoping her voice was steadier than her heart, which was beating wildly.

"I've never seen a cat do that. Have you? Like a dog!"

Elsby shook her head.

"The poor thing had no collar." Aunt Verity paused. "Nor clothes."

Elsby turned and stacked more cans, one at a time, as slowly as if they were made of delicate glass.

"I should start leaving some cat food out for it on the porch," Aunt Verity continued. "We'll get some at the grocery store next time."

"Don't you think cats would prefer, like . . . real food?" said Elsby, glancing over her shoulder. "Um, fresh fish or something? Or . . . I don't know . . . liver?"

Elsby swallowed hard. The cats' secret made her throat itch, like she was allergic to it.

Aunt Verity looked at her curiously. "*Liver?* Very considerate, Elsby. It is something to ponder, isn't it, what cats must think of the canned food we devise for them? If only we could ask them."

Elsby nodded. "If only."

CHAPTER SEVEN

The Banquet

All afternoon Elsby waited for the cats to appear. She drifted around the garden pretending she was looking for rabbits. Her mother texted a few times, and Elsby wrote back on the tiny keyboard that made her thumbs hurt. Aunt Verity boiled a package of ramen for lunch, and then Elsby went back outside to sketch flowers while Aunt Verity took a nap.

Elsby glared at the windows of the cats' half of the house, and even climbed the first low branches of the peach tree, which was festooned with little yellowish-green pompoms of baby fruit, trying to peer into the first floor. But the curtains were drawn tight. Nothing stirred.

She wasn't sure exactly what she expected, but *something*. Cats napped during the day, but not *all* day. Couldn't they peek through the curtains and wave? Or even invite her inside?

Maybe she had offended them. She thought through their list and what she had bought, worrying she had made a mistake. Or what if some of the money had fallen out of the pouch and the cats assumed she'd stolen it?

Around three o'clock the haze thickened into drizzly clouds, and Elsby gathered up her sketchbook—the rose she'd just drawn was now splotched with raindrops, but the effect wasn't bad—and hurried inside.

By bedtime Elsby was angry. She fumed as she checked her legs for ticks. She glowered at her hands, which were still chafed from the heavy bags. All that risk and awkwardness and discomfort, for what? Not even a *thank you.*

The cats had vanished, as if they had never existed in the first place.

"Typical cats," Elsby muttered to herself.

After she finished the tick check, Elsby sat on her bed. A wave of loneliness washed over her. It was nine p.m., and her great aunt had already gone to her room. Out in LA, where it was six p.m., her mother was at some fancy fundraising dinner.

She scrolled through her phone. Her contacts list was very short. She never really hung out with any kids outside school, besides Helen.

She wanted to tell Helen about the cats—but how? How could she possibly explain it all in a message? Her thumbs hurt just thinking about it.

Anyway, Helen was at a Girl Scouts' sleepaway camp in upstate New York. The staff had locked away her phone on the first day and were only going to return it for one hour each Saturday. She and Elsby were supposed to send each other letters, but Helen hadn't remembered to find out the address for the camp in time to share it with Elsby. So Elsby was waiting to get her first letter from Helen at Aunt Verity's house.

She wondered if she could describe the cats better in a letter. Would Helen even believe her? Or would she think Elsby was just making it all up because she wanted to become a writer?

Not that it mattered, since the cats had clearly used her for groceries and then ditched her, likely never to be seen again.

It was pitch-black outside. Elsby switched off the lamp, then scooted over to the window and pressed her face to the glass. The clouds had cleared to show the many stars in the sky, much brighter than they ever were back at home. They were like spilled glitter on a black cloth.

But no cats.

"You can't just ignore me," Elsby said under her breath.

She poked her head out of her doorway. Down below,

Aunt Verity's light was off. She must have gone to sleep.

Elsby went back to her window and wrenched it open as quietly as she could. From the corner of her eye she thought she saw a small square of paper flutter from the sill. But when she turned, it had already blown away.

She grabbed her flashlight and crept out onto the roof. It was scarier without the cats guiding her. She blotted out thoughts of what would happen if she fell, and quickly shuffled to the cats' window, hoping it would be unlocked.

It slid open easily. The cats' house was as dark as the inside of a pocket.

As she started to lower herself in, something warm and furry brushed against her bare knee. Elsby gasped, and the something yowled.

The next thing she knew, she was on the floor. Someone had slammed the window shut behind her.

A voice hissed, "Hasn't anyone taught you to knock first?"

That had to be Clarissa.

"You're so terribly late," said someone else—Marzipan. "We were just about to go get you. We worried we'd offended you—"

"Or that you'd decided to betray us," interrupted Clarissa.

"I'm so confused right now," said Elsby, fumbling to switch on the flashlight.

Clarissa and Marzipan crouched in front of her, both wearing floral Victorian dresses and covering their eyes with their paws. Behind them glowed the four tiny cat beds with their lace canopies and small embroidered pillows.

"Can you turn off that torture device?" snarled Clarissa.

"For the record, I would never betray you," Elsby said, switching the flashlight off.

"So you say. With cats, what you see is what you get," said Clarissa, her voice acidic in the sudden dark. "But humans are like dogs. They wag their tails, then slink around and steal your dinner."

"Enough, Clarissa," said Marzipan. "Clearly there's been a misunderstanding. Elsby, we are holding a feast of grati-tude in your honor. We stuck an invitation to the banquet into your windowsill, but it seems you didn't get it."

The tiny piece of paper!

"I'm sorry," said Elsby. "I think it might have gotten lost."

"Ugh, Marzipan, when will you ever learn?" said Clarissa. "I *told* you we needed the number for the child's pocket phone—she must have one; they all do these days."

Marzipan let out a long sigh. "Why does it even mat-ter? Our landline is going to be cut off any minute. Rose's credit cards all got canceled and no one is paying the bill," said Marzipan.

"Oh no," murmured Elsby.

"Thank heavens we still have electricity to properly cook. Though no doubt our days are numbered there, too. But for now, the feast," said Marzipan.

Elsby followed Marzipan down the attic steps to the second-floor hallway. A sconce was glowing on the wall, and a door was open. As they passed it, Elsby caught a sight curious enough to make her stop and stare.

The room was full of books and a low, long wooden table jumbled with a bizarre assortment of parchment paper, crystals, and various jars of colorful powders. Above the table was a sign written in spindly ink: TO KNOW, TO WILL, TO DARE, AND TO KEEP SILENT.

Elsby took a step into the doorway.

A red-clawed paw clamped around Elsby's wrist.

"What do you think you're doing? Spying?" Clarissa hissed.

Clarissa let go, sprang in front of her, and reached up to pull the door shut.

"What's that room for?" said Elsby, staggering back and rubbing her stinging wrist.

"None of your business, you snoop," said Clarissa. Her long hair was on end.

"Clarissa, really? Please behave yourself. Elsby is help-ing us," said Marzipan. "I'm sorry, Elsby."

Clarissa snorted, then turned and pranced down the

steps to the first floor, her tail swishing behind her.

"But what . . . what was that room? With all the odd things in it?" Elsby stared at the shut door.

"Clarissa's study," Marzipan said after a pause.

For studying *what*? Elsby wondered. But she didn't say it out loud.

Garlands of wildflowers hung from the kitchen ceiling. Tall candles in fancy brass holders glowed on the table, which was covered in a red-checked tablecloth and weighed down with many dishes of food. An unfamiliar scent wafted in the air.

Horatio and Tappy stood on stools. Each wore an apron and a tall white chef hat. Tappy stirred something bubbling in a pot on the stovetop, while Horatio arranged pieces of broccoli on plates on the counter.

"Welcome, welcome," said Horatio, glancing up. "Pardon us, we're almost ready."

"We don't usually eat this early," said Clarissa.

Elsby glanced at the clock above the doorway. It was nine-thirty.

"Rose let us eat dinner at half past four, as we preferred," sighed Tappy.

"Half past four in the *morning*," added Clarissa. "The proper hour. We're making an exception for you."

"Um, thanks," said Elsby.

"Here, serve yourself," said Marzipan, handing Elsby a gold-rimmed porcelain plate. "Don't be shy."

Elsby selected a few scoops from the dishes Marzipan showed her—everything was various shades of greenish brown—then followed Marzipan into the dining room.

More flowers dangled from the ceiling, and the long table was set with place mats, goblets, and twinkling silver candlesticks. Elsby sat down where Marzipan gestured. It was the only chair without an extra-high cushion on it. Soon the rest of the cats filed in, holding their heaping plates.

The cats hopped into the chairs, closed their eyes, and bowed their heads. Elsby copied them, keeping one eye open.

"Thank you, O mysterious cosmos, for this fine meal, and for the beneficent help of our guest, Elsby," murmured Marzipan, her paws pressed together. "Amen."

"Amen," chorused the other cats, opening their eyes.

"Now I propose a toast to our dear Rose," said Tappy, raising her goblet.

"To Rose!" cried the cats.

Elsby cautiously took a sip when everyone else did. The cup was full of water.

"Now," said Marzipan. "We eat."

Elsby took a bite. Broccoli? Maybe. It was dusted in a heavy coating of something that reminded her of freshly cut grass. She swallowed and tried not to make a face, then sampled some of the other lumps. Several of them were definitely liver. One was probably mashed potato, but it was green. Everything Elsby tried had the same herby taste she couldn't quite place.

"So, what do you think, Elisabeth?" Horatio looked at her from across the table. His eyes were oddly glassy.

"Um, there's such an . . . unusual flavor. What kind of spices and stuff do you cook with?"

"Everything starts with a base of catnip," Tappy said in a slightly dazed voice.

"Wow," said Elsby, trying not to gag.

She managed to choke down a few more bites, and then pushed the rest around with her fork, hoping her hosts wouldn't notice.

After the cats had thoroughly licked their plates clean, Tappy went to the kitchen and returned carrying a copper tray glittering with cut-glass bowls full of what she said was vanilla pudding.

Elsby braced herself as she took her first polite spoonful. She was relieved to discover that the pudding had nothing more added to it than whatever was in the packets she had bought at the grocery store.

"Thank you," said Elsby when all the pudding bowls were empty and the others seemed to be emerging from their state of catnip-induced euphoria. "May I help with the dishes?"

"Oh, please, no. You've done enough. We don't know where we would be without you," Marzipan said.

"Besides hungry," said Horatio.

"We were in dire straits," said Tappy.

"I don't mean to be nosy but . . . doesn't Rose have any family or anybody to take you in?" Elsby asked.

"This era we live in!" cried Tappy. "Families, cast to the four corners of the earth! No one feels any responsibility for anyone else."

The words were salt sprinkled on a wound Elsby always kept covered.

"No, Rose didn't really have any human family," said Marzipan. "She got married young, but her husband died soon after the wedding. She was so heartbroken, she never could bring herself to remarry."

"Poor Rose," said Tappy.

"She did have a pair of nieces," said Clarissa. "Dreadful, greedy, tail-pulling children—Ashley and Tiffany."

The other cats shuddered.

"They're adults now. We haven't heard from them," said Horatio.

"May we never," said Tappy, squeezing her eyes shut.

"Oh, yeah. They're feuding over the property," said Elsby, recalling what her great-aunt had said. "They have to go to court. Aunt Verity seemed to think it would take a long time to resolve."

"Thank heavens!" said Marzipan.

"Let's not discuss the nieces," said Tappy in a shrill voice. Her whiskers trembled, and her eyes were still shut. "Please! It will give me nightmares."

"Ashley visited once many years ago," Marzipan whispered as she draped one arm around her sister. "We had to hide in the attic in case we accidentally started talking. But we could hear everything she said. She kept complaining that the house smelled like kitty litter."

"As if we use litter!" huffed Horatio.

"Uh . . . what do you use?" asked Elsby, hoping it wasn't rude to ask.

"We're toilet-trained of course. Just like you—or at least I hope you are," said Clarissa.

"What about your family, Elsby? Why are you staying here with your great-aunt?" asked Horatio.

"Well, my mom had to go to Los Angeles for work," said Elsby. "And I couldn't go with her."

"What about your father?" asked Horatio.

Three pairs of round cat eyes stared at Elsby. In the silence, Tappy slowly opened hers again, too.

"He's not in the picture," Elsby said finally. It was her stock response to a question she dreaded. "I never see him."

Her father was an artist who lived in France, where he was from, and where he was married to someone else and had another family. With other children, ones Elsby had never met. He sent her mother money sometimes, but he had "chosen not to be involved further," as her mother put it.

Elsby knew other kids with parents who did not live together. But she didn't know another child whose father had "chosen not to be involved further"—which really meant he had decided to pretend Elsby didn't exist. The whole situation was so embarrassing that Elsby hated telling anyone. Even Helen. Even these cats.

"Stupid man," said Clarissa after a long silence, and for the first time, Elsby thought she might like her a little bit.

"So how can you all . . . talk?" asked Elsby, trying to change the subject. "You still haven't told me."

The cats exchanged mysterious looks. Marzipan slowly wiped her mouth, and then put down her napkin. "Rose had a . . . strange past."

"Lots of people did who were young during the nineteen-seventies," said Tappy, a little defensively.

Elsby thought back to what she knew of that era. "Was she a hippie?"

"More like a spiritual seeker," said Marzipan. "At least that's what she always said."

"Let's be frank. She was a hippie," Clarissa said.

"Right. Well, it wasn't all tofu and bell-bottoms for our Rose," Marzipan said. "She got involved in . . . magic."

"*Real* magic," said Horatio. "The kind with ceremonies, and chants, and lots of candles and incense."

"Dangerous stuff," murmured Marzipan.

"It was the good kind of magic," interrupted Tappy. "She was a very ethical person. She wasn't a wicked witch."

"She wasn't a witch at all," said Clarissa. "She was a magician. There's a difference."

"What's the difference?" asked Elsby.

"A witch meddles in witchcraft. Simple spells, sometimes pleasant and sometimes rather nasty. You know, broomsticks and herbs, love spells, petty curses, that kind of thing," said Clarissa. She waved a paw around dismissively, as if none of that was very impressive. "A magician—a mage—practices *magic*. A mage draws on the forces of the cosmos to change minds—and sometimes matter."

"But just because Rose meant well . . . " Marzipan trailed off, and the other cats turned to stare at her.

"Rose *always* meant well, Marzipan," said Tappy.

"Isn't there a saying that the road to hell is paved with good intentions?" said Marzipan.

"Rose is *not* in hell. She's in heaven, or on her way there, and someday—"

"Of course, Tappy," said Marzipan. "Of course she is. And I hope we meet her again. It's just—"

"Magic *is* dangerous," said Horatio. His whiskers twitched. "Don't let anyone tell you it isn't."

"I won't," said Elsby, unsure what else to say.

"Which is why it would be better if none of us were involved in it," murmured Marzipan. "It's not safe."

"Speak for yourself," said Clarissa, leaping down from her chair at the table and onto an overstuffed armchair in the corner of the room. "Wimps," she muttered.

"Did Rose ever try . . . whatever she did to all of you . . . on anyone else?" asked Elsby. "Like, I don't know, some squirrels or something?"

"No, never. We were her dearest, most precious companions. Her only cats," said Tappy.

"Oh. Well, what I meant is, um . . . are there any other—well, any other *cats* like you? Like, talking cats that another magician enchanted?" asked Elsby.

"Rose had heard rumors about an Italian sorcerer . . . and some weird happenings in London a long time ago. . . . " said Marzipan, glancing at Clarissa, who was studying her manicured claws. "And of course, Japan is brimming with stories of odd magical cats. But really we don't know. I don't think Rose knew any others."

"Rose worked at the Snipatuit Athenaeum. Have you been there yet?" asked Clarissa, looking up at Elsby.

"My aunt mentioned going there tomorrow maybe. It's some kind of library?"

"Yes. A *strange* library." Clarissa smiled, flashing all her teeth. "Elisabeth, have you heard of Algernon Endicott?"

"Kind of?" said Elsby, recalling his hostile iron gaze when

she passed by on her way to the grocery store. He didn't seem like a very nice person, at least not in statue form.

"He owned a bunch of textile mills in the eighteen hundreds and got very rich," Horatio said. "He used all that money to pursue the study of magic and collect occult objects from all over the world."

"Then he built the Athenaeum as a general library for members, full of regular books. It was the fashionable thing to do back then if you had oodles of cash," Clarissa added.

"Upstairs he kept a room just for his magical books and tools. Scrying stones, crystal balls, that sort of thing," Horatio said.

"Rose, in her early days working at the Athenaeum, discovered one particular book in that room," said Clarissa. "A book which had long ago been written by a famous and talented—"

"And wicked," muttered Marzipan.

"—magician who lived during the Renaissance period in England."

"A *wicked* magician who wasn't a very kind person," said Marzipan. "Many of the other spells in that book are evil."

"No one ever said being *kind* got you power," said Clarissa. "Or safety. A lesson you might want to learn eventually, Marzipan. Anyway, Rose was looking through this book and discovered a very special spell."

"'To Maketh Thee Cat Familiar Speak and Live as Man,'" whispered Tappy, leaning her elbows on the table.

"Or woman," said Clarissa.

"One night soon after, on the evening of the winter solstice, Rose packed us up in our cat carriers and took us to the special room in the Athenaeum tower," said Horatio. "I'm not sure what she thought would happen. But she did her various spells to create the conditions for magic—then recited the enchantment."

"And then . . . we spoke," said Tappy.

"Dear Rose almost had a heart attack," said Horatio.

"Literally," said Marzipan.

"We haven't shut up since," said Clarissa.

"You in particular, Clarissa," said Marzipan.

"Hrmph," said Clarissa.

"Rose quickly recovered," said Tappy. "She took such good care of us. She made us our clothes—she loved sewing! She could sew and weave and knit anything."

"And she taught us to read," said Marzipan.

"She bought us the best food," said Horatio.

"And four times a year she renewed the spell. If only the cost hadn't been so high . . . " Tappy sighed. "I just wish Rose's life had been longer, too."

A look of sorrowful unease came over the faces of the cats when Tappy said this—all except Clarissa, who smiled grimly.

From the parlor's grandfather clock came the sound of eleven deep chimes.

"It's so late," murmured Elsby. "I should go."

What if Aunt Verity woke and looked for her? Or what if her mother called because of some kind of cataclysmic Californian emergency, like a wildfire or a mudslide? Elsby had left her phone on her nightstand.

She stood up, wondering if Los Angeles got tsunamis.

The cats nodded and slipped off their chairs, coming to swarm around her knees.

"Thank you for dinner," said Elsby, looking down.

"We are grateful," said Horatio.

"Also we have another job for you," said Clarissa.

Elsby blinked and forced herself to stop thinking about extreme natural disasters.

"More groceries?" asked Elsby.

She dreaded returning to Roy's Farm & Food Mart for another absurd amount of liver.

"No," said Marzipan.

The cats glanced at one another.

"Are we really going to tell her so soon?" whispered Horatio.

"Not that one yet," said Clarissa. "Books."

"Right. Lots of books," Marzipan said. "It will be fun for you, Elsby!"

CHAPTER EIGHT

Penelope

The Snipatuit Athenaeum was a small castle made of dark red brick studded with crisscrossed diamond windows. It heaved with turrets and towers and curling ironwork along its many peaked roofs and eaves. Even the letters carved in the wooden sign stuck in the lawn looked medieval.

Elsby knew there were libraries just as grand and interesting in New York, but they got lost amid the jumble of other buildings. Her local branch in Brooklyn was, sadly, just a leaky gray concrete box from the nineteen fifties. The roof in the children's room was always under repair, making life difficult for the librarians. The only thing going for the place was that it was full of books and helpful people. The building itself had no soul.

The Snipatuit Athenaeum was different. Elsby stared up at it in awe.

It was Friday afternoon. After her great-aunt's volunteer shift ended, she had picked Elsby up and driven the few short blocks to the Athenaeum, parking on the street outside.

"Fancy, eh?" said Aunt Verity, leading Elsby up the front walk. "Algernon Endicott went for all the bells and whistles building this place. Fortunately, being a member isn't so expensive. I felt it was worth it to join when I moved here."

The front doors were made of dark wood inset with two curved windows, their glass stained and set in the shape of a pair of red roses, thorns and all, flanked by a pair of black ravens.

Copper dust motes swirled in the beams of red-rose light streaming through the lobby windows. There was a worn Persian rug on the floor, and an empty coat-tree warming its limbs above a silver radiator. It felt more like someone's home than a library.

"Children's is in the far back," said Aunt Verity, opening the second set of double doors. "I'm going to the cookbook section. Let's meet back here in twenty minutes, all right?"

"All right," said Elsby.

Elsby stepped into a soaring room with stone floors

and a strong scent of damp paper. Bookshelves lined the walls, and thick tables ran down the center. High up near the ceiling hung old woven tapestries of unicorns and dancing maidens.

Clearly the Athenaeum was a magician's castle—not a regular library.

The room was mostly empty, except for a few gray-haired people sitting at the tables reading books and newspapers. Huge potted ferns swayed over a broad desk, where a librarian was clicking the mouse in front of a bulky monitor that looked like the computer version of a medieval relic.

Next to the staircase was a sign in cursive that read "Nonfiction Upstairs." A wrought-iron elevator stood to its side. Guarding it was a rusting silver suit of armor, its helmet topped by a green-feathered plume.

Aunt Verity disappeared up the stairs. Elsby stood near the elevator. She expected someone to confront her about what she was doing there. She had this feeling almost anytime she stepped into a new place.

But no one looked up or even seemed to notice her. She scurried into the knight's shadow, then pulled a tiny piece of paper from her pocket and squinted down at it.

The cats still had a key to the Athenaeum from when Rose worked there, they had explained. But they were far too honorable to sneak in and borrow books without permission. So it fell to Elsby to replenish their reading material.

Slowly she deciphered the cats' spindly threads of cursive.

The Magic Arts in Celtic Britain
The Brothers Karamazov
Sun Signs & Past Lives
Selected Poems: William Carlos Williams
The Tale of Genji
Beowulf
How to Read an Aura

The list continued for a dozen more lines. Elsby's heart sank. She had never heard of a single book on the list except *Beowulf*. She knew that was a very long and old poem about a monster in England. But where would it be shelved? Poetry? Mythology? Fiction?

"Why can't any of these cats be into, like, Stephen King," Elsby murmured, nudging her glasses back up her nose. "Or some kids' books? No one would question me getting children's books."

She spotted a desktop computer hunched between two drooping aloe plants on a table nearby. "Digital Card Catalog" read the handwritten sign overhead. She knew how to use it from school. She headed over with a sigh.

* * *

Elsby finished collecting *How to Read an Aura* and *Sun Signs & Past Lives* from the section labeled Religion, Magic, & the Occult upstairs. Her arms were already full with several novels. She had managed to find *Beowulf* shelved under British Literature. When she turned the corner toward Poetry to get the last few books on the list, she froze.

A girl her own age, with a face as round as the moon, leaned against the stacks peering into a book called *Gothic Poets of the 19ᵗʰ Century: A Survey*. She wore a long black dress and tall black boots. Her olive skin was daubed with what looked like blush on her cheeks, and her dark brown eyes were rimmed in black kohl eyeliner. Her very straight, shiny black hair was cut in blunt bangs that brushed the tops of her large silvery-rimmed glasses.

Elsby turned around and tiptoed away. The cats would have to do without *Selected Poems: William Carlos Williams* and the other poetry books they had listed. Elsby was far too shy to speak to someone who looked so cool, even just to say, "Excuse me," and reach for a book.

"I cannot believe this. Are you really about to check out *Beowulf*? And *Sun Signs & Past Lives*?"

Elsby glanced back. The girl was pointing at the stack of books in Elsby's arms. Without waiting for a reply, the girl stepped closer and squinted to scan all the titles.

"Seriously! Are you *reading* all these?" She ran one ring-heavy finger down the spines. "Spirits alive! Even *How to Read an Aura?* And *A Foolproof Plan to Rid Yourself of Poltergeists?* You like both occult books, *and* poetry and literature. Seriously?"

"I . . ." Elsby wasn't sure how to reply.

"I swear it feels like all the other kids in this town are just watching TV all day or staring at their phones. How have we never met before?" She lifted her finger from the books and pointed at Elsby. "You don't go to Roger Williams Middle School, do you? Wait. You can't still be in *elementary* school?"

Elsby shook her head vaguely.

The girl narrowed her eyes. "You go to St. Agatha's, then. Wow, I'm jealous. That old building of yours has got to be haunted. I tried to get my parents to agree to send me there just for the chance to ghost hunt."

"Um, no, I don't go there," said Elsby. It took enormous effort for Elsby to form the words and then haul them from her mind through her mouth.

"Homeschooled? Ugh, I would love to be homeschooled."

"No, I—"

"Wait! Are you . . . " The girl took a step forward and poked Elsby's arm with one sharp burgundy nail.

"What was that for?" said Elsby, stumbling back.

"Sorry. I was checking to see if you were a ghost. Or some other kind of entity from the realm of the etheric, like one of the fay." She appeared to notice the bewildered expression on Elsby's face and added, "Fairies. Real fairies are big and look just like you and me. They're not sweet, either. All that Disney Tinkerbell stuff is fake. There are some good books here on the subject."

"No, I'm not a ghost, or, um, a fairy," said Elsby. "I'm not from Rhode Island at all. I'm just staying with my aunt who lives in Snipatuit. I'm from Brooklyn."

"Oh. Cool. Well, how long are you visiting?"

Elsby shifted the books in her arms. Back at home, she tried to get by without really talking to other kids, except Helen. She felt rusty and winded, like when the track unit started in PE and she had to run laps around the gym after months of managing to lurk undetected at the edge of the room during soccer drills and aerobics.

"A week or two." She wondered if the girl would remark on how strange it was for her to check out so many books for so short a visit.

She didn't seem to notice. Instead she whipped out her phone.

"Let's hang out while you're here. I volunteer at the Athenaeum a few hours a week. Gets me free membership. The rest of the time I'm home, either reading or just plain bored out of my mind. Sometimes

I go to the cemetery, just to wander around."

"Wow. Cool," said Elsby. She stopped herself from adding how terrifying it sounded to hang out in a graveyard.

"What I'm saying is, I have a lot of free time, and we like the same books. We should be friends. My name is Penelope Peres. The Portuguese spelling—*p-e-r-e-s*. What's yours? And your number?"

Elsby reeled off her name and her phone number, while Penelope's thumbs zigzagged across her screen.

"Sent," said Penelope, looking up.

Elsby heard a muffled *ding* from her tote bag. She reached in and switched off the phone's sound.

"It's interesting that you volunteer here," said Elsby.

"Yeah. Tuesdays and Thursdays. It's not as fun since . . . well, my favorite librarian passed on a few months ago."

"Rose?" said Elsby, this time without thinking.

"You *knew* her?"

"She's my great-aunt's landlady and neighbor. I mean, was." Elsby blushed at her mistake. "I'm sorry for your loss."

"Thanks." Penelope gazed somewhere beyond Elsby's shoulder as a thin rim of tears gathered along the edge of her eyelids. "I don't think any of us are ever truly *lost*. Souls simply travel beyond the veil, to the next world," she continued, her voice a shaky whisper.

"Beyond the veil." "The next world." A shiver went

down Elsby's spine. She clutched the books more tightly.

"I've thought I felt . . . " Elsby trailed off.

"Yes? Go on." Penelope stared at her with eyes bright as a bird's.

"I've thought I felt Rose's presence a few times."

"Oh, of course! If anyone could come visit us from the other side, it's Rose. I wish she would come see me."

Elsby shuddered slightly. No matter how nice Rose was, dead or alive, Elsby's own preference was to live a completely ghost-free life.

"Um, Rose seemed really great. Like, she was really kind and special," said Elsby, hoping to change the subject.

Penelope nodded and pulled an actual cloth handkerchief from her pocket. It was edged with lace and embroidered with tiny flowers in one corner. "Indeed, she was both those things." She dabbed her eyes and carefully refolded the hanky before putting it back in her pocket.

Elsby watched with envy. Salvation Army had an antique handkerchief bin, but Elsby's mother didn't let her buy them. She was convinced other people's snot never completely washed out, even after a hundred years.

Penelope shoved *Gothic Poets of the 19th Century: A Survey* back into the shelf and turned to Elsby. "Hey, do you want to see Rose's favorite room? It's kind of a secret—only open to visitors sometimes—but I have a key and permission to go there."

"Um—" Elsby thought of Aunt Verity. It had to be close to time to meet her.

"Or not." Penelope stood a little straighter and tipped up her chin, frowning. "But I thought someone who is into *How to Read an Aura* would want to see the Room of Enchantment."

"Oh! The Room of Enchantment? The cats—" Elsby stopped herself just in time.

"Cats?" Penelope asked, tipping her head quizzically.

"Nothing. No cats," said Elsby. "I—I have to meet my aunt downstairs soon."

"It'll just take a minute. It's one of the coolest places in all of Snipatuit. All of Rhode Island, really. No—scratch that. All of New England. All of America!" Penelope grinned and spread her arms wide, revealing voluminous black lace dangling from her sleeves. It made her look like a fancy bat.

"Well . . ."

"Oh, come on. Live a little!"

Penelope led Elsby between bookshelves striped with golden beams of light and then up a dark, spiraling set of stone steps that ended in front of an arched door. Curling black hinges grasped the wood like long-fingered hands. Penelope pulled a silver key out of her pocket and twisted it into the lock. "Rose trusted me with this, and no one has asked for it back yet," she said.

The door creaked open and Elsby gasped.

The room had seven sides, four of them set with small round windows. Bookshelves filled the spaces in between, along with old wooden tables that crouched on monstrous legs carved to look like a lion's. On the floor was a black-and-white tile mosaic in the shape of an odd symbol, a crescent moon with horns and other looped lines coming out of it.

Elsby took a few steps into the room. Its domed ceiling was painted a brilliant deep blue—the color of the sky a moment after sunset—and was dotted with constellations of gold and silver stars. It was beautiful, and it made her forget the uneasy feeling that had crept over her as she had crossed the room's threshold. There was something familiar about the place that she couldn't quite put her finger on.

"This was Algernon Endicott's Room of Enchantment. He practiced magic spells here." Penelope wiggled her fingers and eyebrows. "He was a *very* gifted magician. And not the rabbit-in-a-hat-party-trick kind—he practiced real magic."

Penelope frowned and stared at Elsby as though she was used to being mocked on this point. But Elsby just nodded. She no longer doubted the existence of magic.

Penelope shrugged. "I've been trying to channel him from beyond the grave. No luck so far."

Elsby sniffed. The room smelled different from the rest of the library—spicier. Elsby remembered the scent that poured from the tables of the sidewalk incense sellers near Union Square in New York.

"He collected occult literature, and these are all his most important books," Penelope continued, walking over to one of the tall shelves and running her hand along the row of leather spines.

The room filled with a crackling sound. A warped voice echoed around the ceiling chanting, *"Elsby MacBride. Elisabeth MacBride."*

Elsby screamed and dropped several of the books.

"Come to the front desk, Elsby MacBride."

"It's a loudspeaker, silly." Penelope pointed to the curved metal box over the doorway. "We'd better go, I guess."

"There she is! Oh, thank goodness. Elsby, I was so worried. You weren't answering your phone," said Aunt Verity.

Aunt Verity stood by the circulation desk with one hand on her chest. The librarian with the very old computer stared at Elsby from over the top of the monitor. All the gray-haired people at the long tables peered over their newspapers and books.

"I'm really sorry." Elsby wished she knew the magic

spell for melting into the floor.

"She got a little lost, but I helped her," said Penelope.

"Much appreciated, Penelope," said the librarian.

"Thank you, dear," said Aunt Verity. "Your family runs the Bubble Palace, don't they?"

Red rushed up Penelope's cheeks.

"The *Bubble* Palace?" said Elsby.

Elsby imagined a place like the Snipatuit Athenaeum, but instead of a medieval castle full of books it was—what? Made of soap bubbles? Rhode Island *was* strange.

"It's our local laundromat and dry cleaner," said Aunt Verity. "And a very good one at that. Impeccably clean, and it's run by the loveliest staff—Penelope's parents."

Penelope scrutinized the screen of her cell phone, silent and frowning. It was clear she did not want to discuss the Bubble Palace.

"Are those the books you're getting?" said the librarian, gesturing to Elsby.

Aunt Verity's eyes fell on the giant stack in Elsby's arms.

"My dear, I admire your ambition, but . . ."

Elsby gritted her teeth. What could she say? She hated disappointing the cats. And this giant stack wasn't even all the books the cats had requested.

Aunt Verity trailed off. She seemed to be considering something.

"Well, it seems you have been quite modest about your reading skills, Elsby. I'm impressed. Let's get these checked out."

Elsby glanced at Penelope, who was still staring at her phone as if it was the most fascinating thing in the world.

It felt awful letting everyone believe a lie. But Elsby didn't want to break her promise to the cats, either.

"Penelope seems like a very nice girl," Aunt Verity said as they drove home. "Glued to her phone, sadly, but very kind of her to guide you downstairs. And to volunteer at the library! Maybe you could meet up with her while you're visiting."

Elsby dug through her tote bag for her own phone. Did such a cool girl actually send her a message? Did Penelope *really*, actually, truly want to be friends? It was hard to believe.

But there it was.

Hello Elisabeth! This is Penelope. Want to hang out this weekend?

Elsby stared at the message. She *did* want to hang out. Very much.

But what would happen when Penelope realized she didn't know anything about poetry, or astrology, or Japanese literature, or whatever else that the cats were into?

And how would Elsby manage to keep the cats a secret?

Elsby tried to imagine staying quiet about them in front of a girl like Penelope . . . and queasiness bubbled in her stomach.

She slowly pressed the buttons to add Penelope's name to her list of contacts.

But she left the text message unanswered.

CHAPTER NINE

The Cats' Quartet

It took Elsby three trips across the roof to cart the books to the cats.

The moon was a crescent-shaped snip of paper high in the dark sky. Elsby was so startled by the scattering of stars around it that she stopped and looked for a while. They were never this bright in Brooklyn.

"I'm sorry they didn't have them all," Elsby said when she'd delivered the last load and crawled through the window.

"We'll survive," said Horatio, who was waiting for her in the dark attic room. He passed the books along to the others, who quickly scurried off with them.

Elsby followed him down the attic steps carrying the last few volumes. The door to Clarissa's study was closed, but as they passed it, she felt a jolt of recognition. Now she knew why the tower room at the Athenaeum had felt so familiar!

Clarissa's room of books and crystals and strange symbols had the same sleepy yet menacing energy. Elsby stared uneasily at the shut door.

Downstairs, the parlor was hushed. Each cat was thoroughly absorbed in a book with more piled around them.

Marzipan, perched on the sofa, glanced up from *Beowulf.* Her stack was the shortest. It looked like Elsby had been able to find just three of the books she'd requested.

Horatio clapped his paws. "It's time to properly thank the child."

All the cats shut their books, except Clarissa. She pressed her face further into *Vampires: A New Look at an Ancient Problem.*

"Clarissa, please," said Marzipan.

Clarissa ignored her.

Marzipan slinked over and wrenched the book out of her paws.

"That was unnecessary," Clarissa huffed.

"You could say the same about your behavior," replied Marzipan.

"It's time for our performance." Horatio turned to

Elsby. "As a small gesture of our gratitude, we would like to entertain you."

"Um, okay," said Elsby.

"Settle in," said Marzipan. "We have to change first."

The cats hustled up the stairs, whispering and muttering. A few minutes later they were back—but they looked totally different.

The cats were now dressed in outfits of luxurious Renaissance finery, like Queen Elizabeth I, with puff sleeves, flowing skirts, laced bodices, and intricate floral embroidery. Each cat, except for Marzipan, carried a small black leather case.

"Wow," said Elsby.

"Wasn't Rose talented?" said Marzipan, pausing to curtsy on the stair. Swathes of shiny evergreen and pink silk swirled around her. "She stitched all of these for us."

The cats gathered in a circle in the parlor and began unlatching their cases. "I hope you like classical music," said Horatio, pulling out the tiniest violin Elsby had ever seen. He was wearing a funny round hat with a giant crimson-red feather sticking out from it.

Elsby wasn't exactly sure she liked classical music, but she *wanted* to be someone who did.

"You better, because Rose didn't bother teaching us any other kind," said Clarissa, who had a slightly larger instrument of the same shape. "I'm on viola."

"Rose had these custom-made for us," said Tappy, blowing scales on her flute.

Marzipan dragged a case taller than she was out of the broom closet under the stairs.

"Marzipan was cursed with the cello, the hulking tank of string instruments," said Clarissa. "Since Rose died, our dear Marzipan has had to keep it downstairs. We simply can't haul the thing up and down the steps."

"I can help," Elsby said, kneeling to open the cello case for Marzipan.

"Thank you, Elsby," Marzipan said when the miniature cello was upright. "We're going to play some of Mozart's flute quartets. Okay, ready everyone? One, two, three . . ."

Elsby settled back on the sofa to listen. The cats were much better than her school's half-hearted orchestra, which couldn't get through any piece of music without a lot of nails-on-chalkboard screeching and awkward rhythms.

Elsby waited until the last notes of Tappy's flute died away, then clapped politely.

"You're supposed to say, 'Encore! Encore!'" said Clarissa.

"Oh. Um—"

"Don't listen to her," said Marzipan.

"I do want to hear more," said Elsby. The music had been at once both jaunty and relaxing, like a meadow on a bright, warm spring day.

"Really?" said Marzipan.

"Really," said Elsby.

"Okay," said Marzipan, shrugging. "We can keep going."

The cats played several more pieces. When Rose's grandfather clock chimed midnight, they stopped and began to put away their instruments.

Elsby stood up. "I should—"

"Wait!" all four cats said in unison.

"Is it time?" whispered Tappy, glancing at the others.

"Elsby, we need your help again," said Horatio. He closed his violin case and hopped over to the sofa.

"If you're willing to take the risk," said Marzipan, looking up from the cello with a worried expression.

Clarissa frowned at her.

"Risk?" Elsby glanced from cat to cat. Only Clarissa would meet her gaze. Marzipan was focusing very intently on buckling her cello case, as if she was performing delicate surgery.

Clarissa leaped onto the arm of the loveseat and stared deeply into Elsby's eyes.

Elsby flinched.

Clarissa smiled, flashing her tiny white teeth.

"All important tasks come with risk," she said. "And you seem like an earnest and good-hearted person. Rare for humans. Not so different from Rose."

Tappy sighed.

"Sit down while we explain. Come along. Make yourself comfortable." Clarissa gestured to the sofa.

Elsby perched on the edge of the cushion.

"Clarissa, you know Rose said to ask a child for help with getting food and things," said Marzipan, looking at Clarissa. "Not *this*."

"What is *this*?" asked Elsby.

"Rose renewed our enchantment four times a year. On the spring and autumn equinoxes, and the winter and summer solstices," said Marzipan as she leaned the cello case against the wall. "With a ceremony of spellwork that she recited in a special room at the Athenaeum."

"The Room of Enchantment?" Elsby asked.

"The one and only," said Clarissa.

"The next renewal is coming up fast," said Horatio. "The summer solstice, at midnight."

"Truly it was fate that brought you to us," said Tappy, clasping her paws together.

"We were considering having Clarissa recite the spell this year, but we didn't know how—or if—that would even work. We've only ever had Rose do it, and she's a human, and not enchanted herself," said Horatio. "Plus she studied magic for years and years. She was an expert."

Clarissa glared at him.

"As is Clarissa," Horatio hurried to add.

"That's the thing I don't get about this whole idea. It's not like anyone can just read a spell and *poof*, it works," said Marzipan. She shook her head. "Magic requires study, and training. And—"

"I will provide all that," Clarissa interrupted. "But we still need a human."

"And then you came along, Elisabeth. Dear Rose was helping us from the beyond!" Tappy sniffed. "I think she must have sent you."

Elsby grimaced. She didn't like imagining that.

"So, we need you terribly much, Elsby," said Clarissa.

"If you agree," murmured Marzipan.

Elsby remembered the uncomfortable heaviness of the Room of Enchantment. Beautiful as it was, she wasn't eager to return—especially not for some kind of mysterious ceremony.

"What happens if I don't?" Elsby said, feeling uncertain.

"We die," said Clarissa.

"Or at least stop being able to speak," said Marzipan.

"Same difference to me," said Clarissa.

"At some point, like everyone else, we must leave this mortal coil," said Marzipan. "But the truth is, we don't know what happens without the enchantment. Rose kept performing the ritual year after year, despite . . . despite the trouble of it. And we kept living and speaking. She was very scared about what would happen if she stopped."

"Our sweet Rose loved us so much," whimpered Tappy.

"This is a chance to save our lives, Elisabeth," said Clarissa.

Saving animals' lives. That was important.

"Okay. I'll do it. How do I help?" Elsby nudged her glasses up her nose.

"What do you know how to do, magically speaking?" asked Horatio.

"Well . . ." When Elsby pictured helping animals in need, it was with things like food and bandages, or finding a home. She knew nothing about magic. But she wanted more than anything to save the cats.

"She can't do any magic, clearly," said Clarissa. "She's a regular old child. But that shouldn't matter. Or at least, not for *us*. We just need her . . . presence."

"I don't know, Clarissa," murmured Marzipan. "It's just—"

"Don't bother your little brain about it, Marzipan," snapped Clarissa. "I'll be handling most of the spellwork anyway. Midnight on the summer solstice is just two weeks from tonight. You can meet us here at eleven, and we'll walk over together."

"You don't have to, Elsby," Marzipan said.

"But she certainly *wants* to," Clarissa interrupted. "Don't you want to help us, Elsby? You aren't like all those awful humans who hurt animals, who dump us at shelters, who let us suffer torture on farms, who—"

"I'm not like those people at all!" Elsby hurried to say. "I'll do anything to help you!"

"That's just what I like to hear." Clarissa smiled again.

Marzipan twitched her whiskers and frowned.

Marzipan was quiet as she walked Elsby up the stairs.

"I'm sorry I could only get three of the books *you* requested," Elsby said, when they reached the attic window. She wondered if Marzipan was upset about it.

"Books?" said Marzipan.

"The books from the Athenaeum?"

"Oh! Sorry. My mind was wandering. Honestly, I knew already that the Athenaeum probably didn't have most of the books I wanted. When she was alive, Rose purchased books for the library so we could borrow them. And she used to let me use her credit card to order more books on the Internet. Ones for me to keep. I just wish I could visit an actual real-life bookstore—you know, in person." Marzipan put her chin in her paw and stared up toward the moon. "Even just once."

"Hey, I have an idea," said Elsby. "Somewhere we could go tomorrow afternoon."

Unlike magic, it was something Elsby knew how to do.

CHAPTER TEN

The Bookstore

It had taken quite a bit of convincing to get Marzipan to even consider the idea of browsing for books at Many Moons. The other cats had agreed she could make the trip so long as she stayed naked and hidden in Elsby's bag.

"It's one thing walking around outside pretending to be a regular cat—but to go into a sophisticated place like a *bookstore*, without clothes! I could almost die," Marzipan moaned the next morning on the way to Many Moons.

Elsby peered into her tote at the wide-eyed cat. The sun was hot but the air was dry, and the sky was a still, dazzling blue, like paint fresh from a tube. The street that led to the shop was almost deserted.

"Maybe you could wear your bonnet, at least?" said Elsby.

Marzipan had insisted on Elsby tucking the hat into the tote bag.

Marzipan breathed a sigh of relief and nodded. "Yes. That's enough, I think, to prevent me fainting from embarrassment."

The cat ducked down and reemerged with a purple floral bonnet on her head. "Much better," she said with a sigh.

The door to Many Moons Books was old and thick with many layers of shiny black paint. A cascade of bells pealed when Elsby pushed it open.

Inside it smelled of paper, beeswax candles, and dust. The bookseller sat behind a cluttered counter near the front window, staring at a fat volume in her lap. A tornado of bobby-pinned red hair swirled around her head. She glanced up, nodded, and looked back at what she was reading.

Elsby pushed her glasses up the bridge of her nose and paused. This was the hard part.

"Um, is it okay if I bring my cat in with me?" said Elsby.

The bookseller glanced up again, this time with a blank look.

"She's an . . . emotional support cat. I promise she won't get out."

Marzipan peered over the side of Elsby's tote bag.

The bookseller raised her eyebrows.

"We're definitely spending money," Elsby rushed to add.

"Oh. I mean, spending money is not a requirement to come in," the bookseller said, seeming to recover from her surprise. "We actually have a bookstore cat, too—Pumpkin Ann."

She pointed to a plump orange tabby snoozing on a green velvet cushion in the sunniest part of the window-sill. At the sound of her name, Pumpkin Ann opened one lime-green eye.

"Pumpkin Ann is fine with other animals, but please don't let your cat out of the bag." The bookseller smiled. "No pun intended."

"I would never," said Elsby.

Marzipan stretched her head up higher and looked around.

The bookseller squinted. "Wait. Is that cat wearing a *hat?*"

"Uh. Yeah. She loves . . . bonnets."

"Wow. Pumpkin Ann would draw blood if I tried to put a hat on her. What's your cat's name?"

"Marzipan," said Elsby.

"Like the almond paste? Cool. I think it's an under-rated dessert."

Marzipan ducked and pressed Elsby's arm with her paw. It was a gesture that clearly meant *shut up and hurry.*

"Where's the poetry section, please?" asked Elsby. She pushed at her glasses again.

"That way, against the wall," said the bookseller, pointing.

Elsby hurried to the back of the store, hoping the woman wouldn't follow her. She was relieved when the phone rang.

"This place is amazing," whispered Marzipan as she poked her head back out of the bag. "I've never seen so many books in one place besides the Athenaeum!"

Many Moons was on the small side; Elsby had been in libraries and bookshops in New York with ten times more books. She decided not to tell Marzipan that, though.

"Stop. I think this is poetry," hissed Marzipan. She reached out a paw and brushed the spines. "Mary Oliver, Alice Oswald, Octavio Paz, Li Po . . . ! Oh, I want them *all*. What to pick, what to pick," she muttered.

Elsby tried to angle the tote bag so Marzipan could read the higher and lower shelves. She hoped the bookseller couldn't see her.

"Hurry up," whispered Elsby. "Or she's going to start thinking I'm acting weird."

At last Marzipan made her decisions, mumbling arithmetic under her breath. The other cats had given her some money from the stash Rose had left them.

"That translation of Bashō's haikus, definitely, and the

Alice Oswald book, and that complete collected works of Sylvia Plath," Marzipan said. "Oh, and a new copy of *Macbeth*. Clarissa put her claws through the second act of Rose's old one. If only I were rich! I'd spend my whole fortune on books."

"Interesting selections," said the bookseller as she rang up Marzipan's small stack. "I can tell you're really into poetry. We have readings here sometimes, you know. You should look at our calendar and come by."

Marzipan let out a ragged gasp.

The bookseller stared at Elsby's tote bag. "Is your cat okay?"

Elsby peered into the bag. Marzipan's round eyes looked up at her. "Um, yeah. Probably a hairball."

"Seriously. Everyone is welcome," said the bookseller.

"Thanks. I'll consider it." Elsby grabbed Marzipan's books and the change, and fled out the door.

As soon as they were outside, Marzipan poked her head out of the tote bag and asked Elsby for the Bashō book.

"What if someone sees you?" whispered Elsby.

"I just can't wait!" snapped the cat. "Ah, that new book scent. There's nothing like it. Oh, and this translation is great! Listen."

Elsby glanced up and down the street. It shimmered with summer heat. No one was around.

"*Under cherry trees, /* " recited Marzipan, "*soup, the*

salad, fish, and all / Seasoned with petals.'"

Marzipan let out a delighted sigh. "Isn't it perfect? Bashō perfectly evokes a picnic in spring . . . all the petals from the cherry tree coming down in the breeze and mixing with the food. . . . You would never guess it was written four hundred years ago."

"Yes, very nice," Elsby said. "But keep your voice down."

"Do you think there's any way that I could . . . well . . . visit the bookstore to hear a poetry reading?" asked Marzipan. "I know it's probably not a good idea. I just—I haven't told many people this, but I write poetry, too!"

"You do?" Elsby looked down at the cat. She thought that if she could see under Marzipan's fur, she would be blushing.

"Yes. I write sonnets, haiku, free verse. . . . I submit to all the literary journals. Rose used to help me. But nothing's been published yet. Probably never will be." Marzipan sighed. "Our Wi-Fi got cut off right after Rose passed on, so I can't even submit anything anymore. Not that it matters. I don't think anyone really wants to read what I write."

"Well . . . I would love to read your poetry," said Elsby.

"Really?"

"Of course," said Elsby. "You know—I write, too."

"You *do*? Poetry?"

"Novels." Elsby paused. "Well, first chapters of novels."

"I get it. I've written a lot of first stanzas. It's hard, isn't it?" Marzipan closed her book.

"It's so hard," said Elsby.

None of the other kids in Elsby's school actually cared about writing. Not the way she did. No one else thought up characters and plots. No one else drafted first chapters. No one else wanted to *be* a writer. Helen was the closest, because she loved to read and wanted to be a librarian. But Helen didn't "think in plots," the way she said Elsby did. Elsby took it as a compliment, especially considering she had never managed to *resolve* any of them.

Maybe Marzipan didn't think in plots, either. But she seemed to think in poems, and that was close enough.

"I've never known anyone else who enjoyed writing," said Marzipan.

"Me neither. Oh, we have so much to talk about!" Elsby exclaimed, grinning.

But instead of smiling back, Marzipan's furry face crumpled. She began to weep.

"I just never expected . . . I never expected to *like* you, Elsby. Or any human but Rose." Marzipan took a staggered breath.

Elsby was speechless. Marzipan had seemed so unflappable. Why on earth was she crying now?

"And if it goes wrong, after you . . ." Marzipan trailed off with a sob.

"I'm sure there's some way I can still help after I leave," said Elsby. "Maybe I can visit."

Marzipan gasped. "From the other side? It's not guaranteed, Elsby."

"There's a train from New York to Providence, you know. Probably buses, too. I'm sure I can convince my mom to let me visit Aunt Verity. And that means visiting you!"

Marzipan wiped her eyes with her bonnet ties and took a shuddering breath. "I don't think you understand."

"We have plenty of time—"

"How is your health?" Marzipan scrambled up to Elsby's shoulder and peered into her face.

"My *health*?"

"Any underlying conditions? A weak heart? Consumption?"

"*Consumption?*" Elsby said, and shook her head. She had heard the phrase somewhere before. Was that what killed Beth March in *Little Women*?

"The wasting-away disease where you cough up blood? They send people to recover in sanatoriums for it? I guess it's called something else these days." Marzipan sank back down in the bag so just her bonnet poked out.

"I'm perfectly healthy." Elsby frowned. Marzipan was acting strange.

"I guess that's good news. It's just—Clarissa keeps

telling me I'm a worrywort for thinking . . . " Marzipan once again began to weep.

"Oh my goodness," murmured Elsby. "What's actually going on? Are you okay?"

"You're just so nice—and—and—I have to go now. L-l-leave the books on the windowsill. Thank you for everything." With a rip of claws on cotton, Marzipan lurched out of the tote bag. She fled up Silver Crescent, her bonnet flapping behind her.

Elsby staggered up to her great-aunt's steps and sat down. A flock of woolly white clouds was grazing in the blue sky. The air was still.

She fought back the rising taste of salt in her throat. Elsby expected *humans* to act like Marzipan just had— bewildering and disappointing—but not animals. Not cats. Not even talking cats.

Oh well. Poets were known to be emotional. Maybe that was it.

Aunt Verity's yard was quiet. Elsby sat thinking for a long time, until her phone let out a quick birdsong trill.

She hurried to pull it out of her pocket. That specific sound meant one thing—a text from Helen. Finally!

Hey Elsby. What's up? Hows RI? Camp is great. Really hot! 😆
I saw a snake 🐾

You would have been excited becuz it was bleeding + it needed 2

b rescued

We tried to save it but . . . it died 🐍 🪦

I guess this is a bummer story. . . .

Oops. I can only text every Saturday for an hour

Already over!

Sorry, no mail yet. I forgot stamps. . . . Hope you are having fun in

RI!!! 😵

Elsby's heart sank, first about the poor snake, and then because Helen hadn't even remembered stamps. And she forgot to include her camp address in the text, too.

It didn't seem worth it to text Helen back. Not when she wouldn't read it until next Saturday. Anyway, Elsby had the cats to spend time with now.

Or did she?

Elsby remembered Marzipan's strange behavior, and winced.

Her thumb hovered over the keyboard on her phone. She used the little arrow button to scroll up and saw Penelope's message.

Maybe Penelope wasn't too cool to be friends with. And maybe Elsby would be able to keep her mouth shut about the cats and their secret. Maybe she really could make a friend in Snipatuit—a human friend.

She took a deep breath and began to type.

Hi it's Elsby
Sure, let's hang out ☺

And hit Send.

Elsby had just slipped the phone back into her pocket when the phone went *ding*. She fished it out again. Penelope had already responded.

Shall we meet at the Snipatuit Burial Ground tomorrow morning at 10? Your aunt shall be able to give you directions. It's a rather short stroll from the Athenaeum.

Penelope didn't just dress like a Victorian lady; she texted like one, too.

Sounds great, see you then! Elsby typed, and then immediately erased it.

She had almost forgotten. Aunt Verity had mentioned that tomorrow morning she would be taking Elsby somewhere as a surprise.

Elsby looked down at the phone, her thumb growing sweaty on the keys.

Surprises could be risky. What if her aunt was taking Elsby somewhere embarrassing, like a children's museum? It didn't seem like her style, but Elsby hesitated.

Still. Whatever it was, maybe it was worth trying to bring Penelope along.

She looked up as her aunt's car crunched along the driveway. Aunt Verity parked and got out, smiling and waving.

Before she had time to chicken out, Elsby stood. "Could I bring someone with us tomorrow?" she asked.

CHAPTER ELEVEN

Blueberries

"Blueberries! Oh, look, Elsby, we get to pick blueberries!" said Penelope, leaning out the open car window.

Aunt Verity turned down a long, puddle-pocked driveway bordered on both sides by old stone walls. The driveway had three painted wooden signs: "HAWTHORN FARM," "PICK-YOUR-OWN BLUEBERRIES—ORGANIC!," and "PLEASE DRIVE SLOWLY—LOOSE CHICKENS." This was Aunt Verity's surprise trip, and it was so exciting, Elsby felt her heart flutter.

"Be careful, Aunt Verity, there are chickens," she said.

"Oh, I'm watching. Thanks for the reminder." Aunt Verity slowed the car to a crawl. They bumped their way passed a field of half-grown sunflowers on one side and, on the other, a pen of loud goats. Beyond it, nestled in a grove of dark pines, was a tiny, hushed farm stand and a little clearing marked by a sign that said PARKING. Theirs was the only car.

"This is going to be so much fun!" announced Penelope.

"We're lucky they've ripened so much earlier than usual this year," said Aunt Verity.

The air had that magic smell—the one Elsby had noticed the very first day she arrived in Rhode Island. Here it was even stronger, as if a green forest wizard had just swirled through sprinkling mossy spells all around.

A moment later the magic was ruined by Aunt Verity's putrid bottle of bug spray.

"Does it really keep the ticks off?" Elsby held her nose as Aunt Verity doused her ankles and wrists.

"One can hope," said Aunt Verity, wrinkling her nose.

"I'll do my special tick protection ritual, too," said Penelope, rubbing some of the bug spray on her neck. "Here it goes."

Penelope tilted back her huge straw hat, closed her eyes, and spread her arms. The breeze twirled her white sundress around her legs.

"O spirits of the forest and field, protect us as we walk around picking blueberries!" she announced in a commanding voice. She swept her arms down toward the gravel-flecked ground. "O tiny ticks, leave our blood alone!

Believe me, it doesn't taste good! Thank you." Penelope brought her hands together and bowed.

"Hear, hear," said Aunt Verity. "And bravo."

"Does that . . . work?" asked Elsby.

"Well, I made it up. But it's worth a shot." Penelope shrugged.

Aunt Verity nodded. "Things like that often work when they are full of intention and sincerity, Penelope. So it just might."

Elsby looked at Aunt Verity. What did that even mean?

"Exactly," said Penelope, beaming. "Let's go pick blueberries!"

The farm shed was tidy but mostly empty. There was a stack of plastic buckets with long strings and a pile of blue paper baskets. Beside them were a scale and a locked cashbox with a slit in the top.

"Honor system," said Aunt Verity.

They gathered their buckets, putting them crisscross over their chests, and followed the signs through the forest to the blueberry patch. Along the way Elsby kept her eyes peeled for the chickens. She had never met a chicken before—well, not a living one—and she was very curious.

A bank of yellowish sunshine appeared ahead, and then a field with rows of bushy trees about seven or eight feet tall. Shimmering metallic streamers hung on ropes between them to scare the wild birds away.

Elsby squinted at the ground, looking for the berries.

"Here we are, girls," called Aunt Verity, marching ahead to the closest tree. *Plink, plink, plunk.* She plucked berry after berry off the branches and dropped them in her bucket.

Elsby was startled. She'd assumed that all blueberries grew close to the ground, like in that old picture book *Blueberries for Sal.* These plants were enormous. Their leaves glowed emerald green in the sunshine.

"Oh, it's so beautiful here!" said Penelope. "Doesn't it feel holy?"

"Indeed. Orchards are often magical places," said Aunt Verity, pulling a branch toward her. "Now, let's make sure to stay in shouting distance of one another. And remember not to eat too many!"

"Come on, let's start over here," said Penelope, pulling Elsby to the next row. "I bet I can pick more than you."

Blueberry picking turned out to be a very satisfying game. Elsby searched the branches for berry after berry, rejoicing when she found a good ripe clump. Having Penelope along, chattering endlessly about random things, distracted her from dwelling on how Helen didn't seem to care about staying in touch.

"I wonder where the chickens are," said Penelope when her bucket was nearly full.

"Maybe I can call them," said Elsby. If Penelope could do a tick-banishing ritual, couldn't she try to lure a chicken?

"Go for it," said Penelope.

Elsby swung her bucket around to her back and put her hands to her mouth. "Bok, bok, bok!" she called, trying to remember exactly how chickens sounded in the movies.

Nothing happened.

Then there was a rustle from the next row of blueberry bushes, and a little fat hen with glossy, red feathers appeared. Elsby stared at it in shock.

"It *worked*! Oh, Elsby, forget being a novelist. I think you should be a professional chicken finder," said Penelope.

Elsby crouched down. The chicken shifted her head, staring at Elsby with glittering black eyes.

"If only you could speak, too," Elsby murmured, wishing that all animals could talk, not just the enchanted cats.

After blueberry picking, Aunt Verity drove Elsby and Penelope to a little diner with a green-and-white striped awning. The parking lot was almost full, and inside it was hopping with families and old people, and waiters and waitresses who were dashing back and forth hauling heavy trays loaded with pancakes, waffles, burgers, and milkshakes.

Aunt Verity requested a booth by the window, which overlooked some train tracks and a warehouse. In between was a scrubby stretch of litter-stubbled brambles and trees. Chip bags, soda bottles, beer cans, plastic bags. Elsby looked at all the garbage in despair. Why did people *do* that? What made someone look at a beautiful tree or bush and think it was okay to toss trash at it?

Animals couldn't do math or build cities. But they knew enough not to make plastic garbage and toss it into beautiful bits of nature. Why were humans so dumb?

She couldn't stand it.

"Order whatever you want, girls," said Aunt Verity. "My treat."

"Delightful! Thank you!" said Penelope.

Elsby wrenched her eyes away from the window and scanned the plastic menu, looking for the cheapest thing. That was how she and her mother always ordered. Grilled cheese in the kids' section was less than five dollars.

Elsby slouched down in the booth attempting to look smaller and younger. If only she had put her hair in two pigtails instead of the single braid. Over the past year, waiters had started to frown at her attempts to order the kids' mac & cheese or pizza.

"Don't feel like you have to order whatever is least

expensive, or from the children's menu," Aunt Verity said, as if she had read Elsby's mind. "Choose your own adventure, as they say."

"Thank you!" said Penelope.

"Uh. Wow. Okay, thanks," said Elsby.

She sat up straighter. The menu was suddenly much bigger. After much deliberation, she decided on a hummus and avocado sandwich. Nothing with avocado was ever cheap, but this wasn't *too* expensive. And it came with a side of fries and a salad.

"And you should try an Awful Awful," said Aunt Verity.

"Oh, you should!" cried Penelope.

"Excuse me?" said Elsby.

"It's a classic Rhode Island milkshake," said Aunt Verity, tapping on the back of the menu where the drinks and desserts were listed. "Apparently it comes from the phrase 'Awful big, awful good.'"

"It's like liquid candy," said Penelope.

"Hmm," said Elsby. "Yum."

Penelope ordered a turkey club sandwich and Aunt Verity got a hamburger with fries. Elsby ordered her sandwich, plus a strawberry Awful Awful. Penelope chose a chocolate peanut butter one.

Then Aunt Verity asked both of them about what they were interested in and liked to do. Elsby found the words spilling out of her like water from an uncapped fire hydrant on a hot day.

"I like olden days things. Like old clothes, old furniture, old houses. Old books," she said. "I like gardens, and animals. I want to write novels when I grow up. Except also now, too. When I'm an author someday I'm also going to rescue animals. Which I also want to do now . . ."

Aunt Verity nodded, and asked good questions at the right time, like what Elsby's novels were about.

"Well, the book I keep coming back to over and over is called *Matilda of Sunflower Lane* and it's about an orphan from the olden days—"

"How old?" interrupted Penelope.

"Um, I think the late eighteen hundreds. Like, they had telegrams but not cars yet."

"A very interesting period of time. The Gilded Age," said Aunt Verity.

The waitress returned, plunking three heaping plates down in front of them. "The Awful Awfuls will be up in a minute," she said.

"Can I read it?" asked Penelope.

"Well, I haven't finished it yet. Or any book. I've just written a bunch of first chapters."

The last part sounded so pathetic out loud. Elsby stuffed a french fry in her mouth and looked away.

Penelope didn't seem to notice. "That could be a cool kind of book! Don't you think? A book that's just first chapters of other books. Like some kind of experiment! You could call it, like, *A Bouquet of First Chapters*."

Elsby raised her eyebrows. She had never thought of anything like that before. She wished she had her notebook.

"But really I think you should write a novel set in Snipatuit," Penelope continued between bites of her sandwich. "We have loads of weird stuff here. My favorite is the rumors about the cats."

Elsby took a large bite of her sandwich and tried to chew. Her heart was pounding. She didn't dare look up.

"Oh yes, those cats who wear clothes," said Aunt Verity. "There's a long-haired white one who wears a fancy ball gown. I glimpsed her plucking ripe peaches from my tree last July. And Elsby saw one of the cats her very first day. What was it wearing, dear? A sailor suit?"

Elsby swallowed, nodding slowly. She wanted to ask her aunt more about what she knew—she had clearly seen Clarissa!—but she was too nervous to speak.

"*What!* You saw one and didn't tell me?" said Penelope.

"I mean, I think I saw one. Maybe I need new glasses," mumbled Elsby.

"Ugh. I would *love* to see one. Did it talk? I've heard rumors from other kids that they can talk. Did the one you saw at your peach tree talk, Verity?" asked Penelope.

"Why didn't you tell me before about seeing her?" asked Elsby, her mouth dry.

"The conversation had moved on to other things," said Aunt Verity with a shrug. "And you never mentioned it again."

Penelope leaned back and sighed. "I'm so jealous. I haven't seen anything so cool as that. But maybe Elsby and I can go to my favorite place after this, the Snipatuit Burial Ground. Would that be okay?" She turned to Aunt Verity with a pleading look.

Elsby shivered. She wasn't sure how she felt about graveyards, but she was glad for the change of subject.

"An occasion to contemplate mortality, I see. I suppose that's fine," said Aunt Verity.

Just then the waitress appeared with the Awful Awfuls. Elsby took a sip, letting the amazing sweetness wash over the sour taste of her nerves.

CHAPTER TWELVE

The Burial Ground

The Snipatuit Burial Ground was the same graveyard where Marzipan had waited while Elsby shopped at Roy's Farm & Food Mart. The stone wall surrounding it at hip-height was embroidered with bright orange lichen. The gravestones were thin and brown and tilted at wild angles, like they were trying to cuddle amid the patchy grass and moss.

Aunt Verity waved as she pulled away in the car. Penelope ran ahead, but Elsby hesitated at the curling black wrought-iron gate.

"Oh, Elsby," Penelope called over her shoulder. "You don't have to be so spooked. Ghosts can't really hurt you. At least, not any of these ones."

"Right. Cool," Elsby said as she hurried up the pathway toward Penelope.

"I'll introduce you to my favorite dead people," Penelope said. "Come on!"

Elsby followed Penelope as she pranced between the rows of headstones. They were very old, almost ancient, with surfaces like the rough texture of graham crackers. Many of the stones were so worn, it was hard to see the words carved on them.

"This one first," said Penelope, squatting down beside a thick, small one. Sweet little yellow wildflowers hugged it, and a carved skull with wings stared up at them beseechingly from its top. Elsby could just make out what was chiseled below:

HERE LIES BURIED

SILENCE MAYHEW

(A HOPEFUL CHILD)

DAUGHTER OF MOSES & ELIZABETH MAYHEW

WHO DEPARTED THIS LIFE

THE 7TH DAY OF DECEMBER 1698

AGED TEN YEARS

"That's called a memento mori," said Penelope, running her fingers over the little winged skull. "I wonder what she was like. Silence, I mean. She was only ten when she died. Did she like to make up stories? Did she get to ride horses? Or did Silence have to work all the time, like on her farm or something?"

"Her name was *Silence?* How do you . . . how is that even a girl's name?"

"It says 'daughter,' plus I looked it up. Do you know about the Puritans? They had the wildest names. I mean, most of them were Sarah and John or whatever, *bor*-ing, but others were really out there. Lament, Remember, even a guy called Die-Well. But can you imagine being named *Silence?*" Penelope lovingly patted Silence's headstone.

Elsby decided she would research Puritan names sometime soon. Maybe she could even write a novel set in that time period . . . there must have been a lot of orphans. . . .

While Elsby stared into the distance, daydreaming about another possible book, Penelope kept talking.

"Have you ever wanted to change your name? I really want to change mine. Maybe to Persephone. Do you know about Persephone? *Penelope* means 'weaver,' which is nice and all, but *Persephone* is an ancient Greek goddess of the underworld, and that's much more interesting. Fits me better. I tried it out for a bit last year, but everyone thought I said *Stephanie.*" Penelope exhaled.

"I like Penelope better," said Elsby, which was the truth.

"Well, thanks. I still think Persephone would be better for my professional ghost-hunting career when I finally get it started. Assuming people get the reference."

"Are there really a lot of ghosts here?" asked Elsby.

"There's lots of strange stuff in Rhode Island. Not just sweet stuff like milkshakes with funny names and cats with clothes." Penelope dropped her voice to a whisper. "Do you know about Mercy Brown, the vampire of Rhode Island? Or the *Palatine*, the ship that sank off the coast here and still haunts our waters?"

Elsby shook her head. "Do you know" was Penelope's favorite phrase.

"New York City may have a lot of world-famous stuff, but it can't beat New England for creepiness." Penelope jumped to her feet. "I'll show you a really strange thing. Come on!"

As Elsby followed Penelope up the hill, the headstones gradually grew shinier, straighter, taller, and newer. They reached an area where crosses soared out of sparkling marble slabs, and statues of angels balanced on top of pure white squares. It wasn't any different from the regular old modern graveyard next to a strip mall in Pennsylvania where Elsby's great-great-uncle Raymond had been buried the previous summer.

It was just when Elsby was sure nothing very interesting would happen that the hill dipped down again and she saw a gloomy building in the distance. It was dark gray and about the size of a city bus. It wore a shaggy coat of moss and lichen, and it was shadowed by a cluster of emaciated pine trees.

As they got closer, Elsby saw that the building was covered with sculptures and carvings. Many symbols—similar to astrological signs but not ones Elsby had ever seen before—were etched in the stone sides. Flanking the single entryway was a pair of fierce marble sphinxes.

Above the rusting metal door, large capital letters read:

HERE LIES THE PHYSICAL BODY OF

ALGERNON HOPKINS ENDICOTT IV

Beneath the inscription was carved the same moon-and-horns-and-lines shape as on the floor of the Room of Enchantment in the Athenaeum, and beneath that the same word Elsby had seen written on his statue: *Redibo*.

"This is his mausoleum," Penelope whispered. "I looked up what *Redibo* means. It's Latin for—"

"'*I will return*,'" Elsby said, remembering what Marzipan had said.

"Wow! You know Latin?" Penelope raised her eyebrows.

"Not really," said Elsby. She swallowed hard.

"Spooky, isn't it?" said Penelope.

It was more than spooky. It was terrifying.

"Could we keep going?" Elsby asked, backing away from the mausoleum.

"Sure," said Penelope.

Penelope marched back up the shady hill into the sun, and Elsby scrambled after her, relieved to get away. She followed Penelope toward an area where the gravestones were scattered widely across a prim green lawn.

They stopped in front of a dark pink marker with angels etched into the corners. The ground around it looked freshly disturbed, and in front of it was a cluster of objects: a single bouquet of plastic flowers and three half-burnt white candles in tall glass votives.

"Rose Fairweather's grave!" Elsby whispered, reading the name.

Penelope lightly brushed the top of the headstone and nodded.

"I came with Mrs. Rebello a few weeks ago. She's the library secretary. She brought the flowers, and I got those candles," said Penelope. "I got them at the grocery store. No one else seems to visit. I know she had a husband who died young. So tragic. Do you know if she had any other family?"

Elsby shook her head. "Just a pair of nieces."

"Oh yeah. Mrs. Rebello mentioned them. They didn't even come to the funeral. Can you imagine? Having such a cool aunt, and not even caring? Rose was wonderful. But it seemed like no one loved her."

"Her cats did," Elsby blurted out. Then she threw a hand over her mouth.

"Her . . . cats?"

Penelope turned to Elsby, her thick eyebrows scrunched together.

"Elsby, Rose didn't have cats. I talked to her *all the time* and she never, ever mentioned cats. Who is taking care of them?" Penelope's voice was slow and steady.

"Well, me. Sort of."

"And your aunt?" Penelope looked confused.

"Er . . . no. Aunt Verity doesn't know about them."

Penelope stared at Elsby. She blinked several times, then frowned.

"I—they—well—her cats, are, um . . . really strange," mumbled Elsby.

Elsby's tongue was drier than a bowl of discount kibble.

"Oh, Elsby!" Penelope grabbed Elsby's hands. "How do you know they were really Rose's?" She dropped her voice to a whisper. "Do they . . . talk?"

Elsby felt like she was standing at a fork in a dark road. Two foggy paths branched out in either direction. One way was loyalty to the cats but lying to Penelope and losing her friendship. The other was betraying the cats by telling Penelope the truth—and becoming the coolest girl in history in Penelope's eyes.

Penelope let go of Elsby's hands and squinted. "Elsby?"

"I . . ." Elsby stared very hard at Rose Fairweather's grave and felt like throwing up.

"Wait a minute," Penelope whispered. "The rumors are true. You've talked to them already, haven't you?"

Before Elsby could think of what to say, Penelope added, "You've spoken to them, and now you want to keep them all to yourself."

"No!" said Elsby, looking up. "That's not it. It's that I promised!"

"Promised what?"

Elsby jammed her face into her hands. This wasn't going well. Not at all. "I promised not to tell anyone about them," she said in a very small voice.

"But—but I'm not . . . *anyone*. I'm Penelope. I'm your friend and I knew Rose." Penelope's voice cracked. "And now you've told me about them anyway. Please introduce me to them! Oh, this would be my life's dream, to talk to them. I promise I wouldn't hurt them or tell anyone else about them, or anything. Oh, please!"

Elsby let her hands fall. Penelope looked at her, her eyes wide and shining.

"Okay," Elsby whispered. Thrill and dread ran through her heart. "Come with me."

CHAPTER THIRTEEN

The Spare

Elsby walked as quickly as possible down the cemetery path and out to the street. Every few steps Penelope would remark on something about Snipatuit—a weird historical fact, a startling detail about a ghost in a house they passed—but Elsby found it hard to pay attention.

"I didn't know Rose lived on Silver Crescent!" said Penelope when they reached Aunt Verity's tiny dead-end street. "I think this is my favorite street name in Snipatuit, and maybe top ten in Rhode Island. It's hard to beat Planet Street in Providence. Do you know that it was named after a famous astrological transit in the 1800s? I think it involved Venus. Anyway, I just live on Roger Williams Street, of which there is one in every Rhode Island town. It's so incredibly boring, I could die. Roger Williams was kind of cool, though. Do you know . . . "

Penelope prattled on about the founder of Rhode Island and his unusual commitment to religious freedom. Elsby longed to ask what the other top nine street names of Rhode Island were, but she was too focused on what would happen when she introduced Penelope to the cats.

She had never met anyone else who actually cared about street names. It felt like a meteorite landing on the sidewalk in front of her. Street names, like the names of characters, were one of the parts of story writing that Elsby relished. It was a source of unending disappointment that her apartment in Brooklyn was on boring old Forty-fifth Street, not on a block with an air of magic, like Cortelyou Road or Joralemon Street.

Elsby turned down the stone path to the front porch, her hands clasped tightly in front of her to hide their trembling. Aunt Verity's car was not in the driveway. There was no wind, and everything was very still. High up in the sky a pack of pure white clouds drifted along without a care in the world. Elsby envied them.

"This is it?" said Penelope. "I always *wondered* what Rose's home looked like. This is perfect—cozy as a gingerbread house, but a little bit magical. Like a wizard's gingerbread house."

"The style is called Carpenter Gothic," Elsby managed

to squeak, remembering her conversation with Aunt Verity.

"You like architecture, too!" Penelope exclaimed, clattering up the steps behind her. "Do you know about Newport? It's a town south of here with a *lot* of amazing architecture and old houses and stuff. You can even go inside some of the big old mansions; you just need a ticket. Hey, maybe your aunt could drive us there while you're visiting! My parents are always way too busy with work."

"That would be amazing," said Elsby.

She tried to think positively. After all, maybe the cats wouldn't be too angry? Maybe they would be excited to meet a kid who lived in town. Maybe they just needed a chance to get used to the idea.

"You have to hide, Penelope," Elsby whispered. "I'm afraid the cats won't come out if they see you."

Penelope went where Elsby pointed, pressing herself out of sight against Aunt Verity's doorway.

Elsby knocked at the cats' door once, then again.

What if they didn't answer? She felt odd about climbing over the roof—especially in daylight—with Penelope.

She knocked a third time, and leaned back to glance at Penelope, who stared at her with a hopeful smile. Some of the kohl around her eyes had smudged. She looked a little bit like a raccoon dressed up as a witch for Halloween.

A terrible thought struck Elsby. What if the cats opened the door, but first took off their clothes? And then acted like normal cats?

Penelope would think she was a liar. And who would want to be friends with a liar?

Elsby knocked again, more forcefully. "Please open up. It's me! Elsby! And it's an emergency."

The door's brass mail flap slowly rose, revealing a bluish-gray paw. Elsby stooped down. A pair of copper eyes glowed in the dark opening.

"Horatio! Please let me in," Elsby cried.

The flap thwacked shut and the door creaked open, ripping apart the skein of cobwebs tangled around the frame.

Horatio looked up at her and frowned. Clarissa stood behind him, half hidden by the door.

"You should stick to the window, Elisabeth," hissed Clarissa. "Also, we were asleep—this is our nap time, you know."

Horatio was in his blue sailor suit. Clarissa was outfitted in a yellow taffeta ball gown with enormous sleeves. She wore a complicated headband studded with fake white roses and lace bows that flounced down over her ears. It didn't seem like something you'd wear to take a nap.

Horatio yawned dramatically. "Why are you here?" he

whined. His tail swished behind him. "Clarissa's right, we were *resting*. It's rather rude of you."

Marzipan's worried face appeared over Clarissa's shoulder. "Don't listen to those two, Elsby. Are you all right? What's wrong?"

Elsby didn't know what to say. She scrambled up from her knees, grabbed Penelope, and tugged her toward the cats.

Horatio shrieked, then threw a paw over his mouth. Clarissa pushed him out of the way and tried to slam the door shut. Penelope was too quick for her—she jammed her foot into the doorway and grinned.

"Elsby! How could you?" whispered Marzipan.

"Shh!" the other cats hissed in unison.

"Hello!" Penelope said brightly. "My name is Penelope. I'm Elsby's friend and I am dying to meet you."

The three cats stared up at her, slack-jawed.

"Meow," said Horatio, unconvincingly.

"I thought you all might want to know another kid," said Elsby. It wasn't *quite* the truth, and lying always made her voice go flat and quiet.

"Don't be afraid of me, kitties," Penelope continued cheerfully. "I was friends with Rose, too, at the Athenaeum. I know you can talk, and I want to help you. I live here in Snipatuit. I'm not just visiting like Elsby."

Elsby flinched. It was true—but she didn't like being reminded about it. What *would* happen to the cats when she went back to New York?

Horatio poked his head over Clarissa's shoulder. Marzipan crept around her. Elsby watched Clarissa's angry scowl morph into something close to delight. She whispered something to Horatio, who tilted his head, then shrugged. An uneasy frown rippled across Marzipan's face, and she hissed something at Clarissa.

Elsby caught snatches of what they were saying: "riskier if the effects take right away—" "—but if it doesn't work the first time—" "—a local—" "—arguably *less* dangerous for children—"

There was more muttering, and Elsby heard Marzipan murmur, "You say it's safe, but what if . . ."

Clarissa snarled something Elsby couldn't hear, and Marzipan scowled at the floor, silent.

"Lovely to meet you, Penelope. A friend of Rose's is a friend of ours—especially a child," said Clarissa, turning back to the doorway and beaming up at Penelope. "Come right in."

Elsby and Penelope sat squished together on the small striped sofa in Rose's parlor. Elsby slid her eyes to observe Penelope, who gazed around the room eagerly.

"You are far less shocked by our existence than this other one was," said Clarissa, jutting her chin in Elsby's direction. She flexed her manicured claws. "When we first met, I nearly had to draw blood to get Elisabeth to believe she was awake and not dreaming."

Elsby grimaced.

"I'm always ready to believe in the supernatural. I've been studying magic and mystery forever," said Penelope.

"A most helpful talent in our situation. We are so fortunate to have you here," said Clarissa. A toothy grin slowly spread across her flat, furry face. "Give her a proper welcome, Horatio."

"I'll get some refreshments," Horatio said, scurrying into the kitchen.

"And do bring out the special box of chocolates," Clarissa called.

Special box of chocolates? Elsby frowned. They had never mentioned bringing out any special box of chocolates for *her*.

Marzipan sat quietly on a floral chair, looking at her folded paws. Tappy stared out from behind a half-dead potted fern in the corner. She was too scared of Penelope to come any closer.

Penelope peered around the room, beaming. "So this is where Rose lived! I love her style. So many antiques. But where are her books?"

For the first time, Marzipan looked up. Elsby saw a gleam of interest in her eye. "She kept most of them upstairs. Would you like to see?"

"Sure!" Penelope jumped up.

"Can't I come, too?" asked Elsby.

"Of course, Elsby!" said Marzipan.

"Make it speedy," snapped Clarissa. "I want to chat more with this new arrival."

As they went up the stairs, Marzipan and Penelope babbled about the Athenaeum and various people who worked there with Rose. Elsby trailed behind, unable to join the conversation.

It wasn't much better when they reached what appeared to be Rose's bedroom.

Unlike Clarissa's study across the hall, this room was bright and airy, with cream-colored lace curtains, a lilac quilt on the small bed in the corner, and shelves crammed with books.

"T.S. Eliot!" cried Penelope, zooming in on a very small leatherbound volume. "I love his poems about cats. Some of the others are so hard to understand. But the lyricism!"

Elsby tried to recall what *lyricism* meant. Something about words sounding good together.

Marzipan closed her eyes and clasped her paws together. "'For I have known them all already, known them all: / Have known the evenings, mornings, afternoons / I have—'"

"'—measured out my life with coffee spoons,'" Penelope joined in, completing the line in unison with Marzipan. "I just love that poem."

"What poem is it?" Elsby managed to ask.

"'The Lovesong of J. Alfred Prufrock,'" Penelope said, and not unkindly. She pushed the book into Elsby's hands. "It's hard to understand fully, but I think it's about being brave. Anyway, it *sounds* so cool."

"I've often wished I could open a coffee shop and call it Prufrock's," said Marzipan, sighing. "Because of the coffee spoons line. How perfect would that be?"

"It could be a bookstore-coffee shop!" exclaimed Penelope. "Oh, how dreamy. Working in a coffee shop sounds so fun. I'd learn to make those swirly pictures in the cappuccino."

Elsby knew exactly how *not* fun working in a coffee shop could be. It was what her mother had done before she started being a full-time curator, and sometimes, when bills were tight and freelance jobs were slow, she would still pick up hours at Café Smile in Manhattan. When she did, Elsby had to stay out of the way at a table in the corner practically all weekend as her mother burned her fingers steaming milk for hundreds of espresso drinks.

But she kept quiet as Penelope and Marzipan

chattered. With a sinking feeling, Elsby realized that she had been so focused on the cats rejecting her for sharing their secret, that she hadn't considered something worse.

What if instead both Penelope and the cats ditched her . . . because they liked one another *better?*

Back downstairs Elsby sat beside Penelope on the sofa, sipping the mint tea Horatio had brewed and eating the chocolates they'd brought out for Penelope. Twice in a row Elsby had chosen the dreaded cherry liqueur. She tried nibbling around the gross filling, but the chocolate itself was flaky and stale.

The cats peppered Penelope with questions about her time volunteering with Rose at the Athenaeum, and where she lived, and what she was interested in. Then they began discussing magic.

Elsby stared into her cup of weak, puddle-colored tea and started daydreaming about her novels. Maybe Sir Peter Cabbage in *Midnight at the Half-Moon Hotel* could save some cats from an evil magician. But why was the magician after them?

"You are definitely better versed in these matters than Elsby," said Horatio.

Elsby looked up when she heard her name.

"You can be the extra one, Elsby," said Clarissa, turning to her. "Having two human souls there might work even better."

"Clarissa knows what she's doing. It's not personal," added Horatio.

"Wait, what? Can someone explain what's going on?" Elsby asked, bewildered. She glanced from the cats to Penelope, who was staring so intently at Clarissa that she didn't notice Elsby's pleading look.

"Penelope will do the enchantment ceremony instead of you," Horatio said. "Thank you, Penelope." He nodded his furry head in her direction.

"I hope that's okay, Elsby. You aren't upset, right?" Penelope said, turning to her. She was biting her lip.

"I mean, no. Of course not. But . . ."

"It's for the best, Elsby. Maybe—maybe Penelope will be able to handle it better. More safely," said Marzipan.

A sunburn-like flush heated Elsby's cheeks. Did the cats think she was dumb?

"Is the spell . . . dangerous?" asked Penelope.

The cats exchanged looks.

"Well, we ought to warn you, it *can*—" Marzipan began.

"*Hush!*" Clarissa hissed like a steaming teakettle. "Why frighten her, Marzipan, when I've assured you over and over that the spellwork is harmless for children? It's perfectly safe. You're scaremongering, and ignorant."

Marzipan fell silent.

"Actually, I like dangerous things!" Penelope rubbed

her hands together. "Besides, since I was eight I've been studying every book on this stuff I could find. I'll be fine."

"Excellent." Clarissa grinned, her pointy teeth gleaming. "Midnight on the summer solstice at the Athenaeum—so very soon. Penelope, you will be our savior. Elsby, though you are merely the spare, try to be on time in case we do need to use you."

Elsby plunked her teacup down on the table and stood up. "Thank you *very much* for the hospitality. Though you should know those special chocolates are stale. We have to go, Penelope."

Penelope blinked. "But—"

"*Now.*" Elsby reached across the sofa for Penelope's cup. She put it down next to her own, more delicately this time, as she felt all the eyes in the room, feline and human, fixed on her.

"Uh . . . okay." Penelope slowly got to her feet. She turned to the cats, her hands clasped together. "Meeting all of you has been the most amazing thing that's ever happened to me. Even better than the time I saw Algernon Endicott's ghost in the broom closet at the Athenaeum. Or at least, I think I did."

"I assure you the pleasure is all ours," Clarissa said.

"I'll see you all very soon," continued Penelope. "Thank you so much for inviting me to the ceremony!"

Elsby marched to the front door. "Come *on*, Penelope."

As she passed Marzipan, Elsby noticed a strange look on the cat's face. Was it guilt? Mixed with . . . relief? She didn't stop to think about it. The noxious smoke of anger and envy filled all the nooks and crannies in Elsby's mind and choked out any other thoughts.

Outside, a heavy, wet wind was blowing. The lids of the garbage cans alongside Aunt Verity's house muttered as though the bins were home to restless ghosts. The sky had turned greenish-gray.

Penelope stood on the porch chattering like a sparrow. "That was *amazing*. The cats are *amazing*. I can't believe Rose never told me. Maybe she was about to tell me when she passed away, you know? She died so suddenly. It's still so sad. Her poor cats! They've been so alone! Until you came along to help them, Elsby!"

Elsby was still smarting from the comments the cats had made about her—and the fact they had kicked her out of her job at their upcoming ceremony, whatever it was. She was too upset to speak.

"I mean, it's so sad, but isn't it also wonderful, Elsby?" Smiling, Penelope reached out and grabbed both of Elsby's hands and squeezed.

Elsby pulled Penelope down the steps and away from the house, then shook off her grip. An awful taste was rising in Elsby's throat, like salt and vomit.

"And they *need* me, too. Or, I mean, us. But me especially, since you are going back home soon," Penelope said.

Home. Elsby felt tears brim against her lids. She missed her mother, and her apartment, and even Helen—Helen, who hadn't bothered to write.

"That black cat Marzipan is a scaredy cat," continued Penelope. "The enchantment ceremony can't be *that* dangerous. Clarissa said it was safe. And anyway, like I said, I've read almost all the books. I know all about the history of—"

Elsby threw her hands over her ears. "Please shut up!" she shouted.

Then she blushed, dropped her hands, and hurried down the stone pathway toward the road.

"Uh-oh," said Penelope. "Maybe I forgot to say thank you. My mom always complains that I forget to properly express gratitude. Thank you! Thank you! Thank you so much for introducing me to them. Isn't it amazing? I still can't believe it. *Talking cats!*"

Penelope's voice thrummed behind her as Elsby rushed along Silver Crescent. "I promise I won't tell anyone. I can keep secrets. Is that it? Besides me being rude, I mean. I really am sorry. But seriously, you can trust me. I know I talk too much, but honestly people don't even listen to me. You seem kinda mad. Is it because they are having me do the ceremony?"

Elsby stopped. *Was* that it? Not really. She hadn't even wanted to do any magic for the cats. It was too disturbing, and it felt dangerous.

What mattered was that *they* didn't want her to, either. The cats preferred Penelope, just like Penelope clearly preferred them.

"It's only because I know more, Elsby. Right? Like, it makes sense. It's not personal."

Elsby whirled around. They were at the corner of Silver Crescent and Pewter Lane. She felt embarrassed about losing her temper—about everything. And most of all, she was worried that neither Penelope nor the cats would care about her anymore.

"I met them first," said Elsby, because she felt she had to say something but couldn't say anything close to the truth.

"Oh no. You *are* upset. Please don't be! Seriously. Of course you met them first, but they need me. After you leave Snipatuit, what will they do?"

"*I* was first. They wanted to meet *me*. They chose *me*. And *I'm* going to help them. Me."

Elsby spoke much louder than she meant to. She held her breath, and cringed, worrying Penelope was going to shout back at her.

But Penelope didn't. Instead she frowned, and looked puzzled.

"But . . . you're going back to New York soon. How are you going to help them from there?"

Elsby didn't know what to say.

"Also, I don't know how to put this exactly. Don't take offense, okay?" said Penelope.

Elsby braced herself. No one ever said *don't take offense* unless what they were about to say was going to hurt.

"It's like . . . it's like you want the cats to be your pets," said Penelope. "But they're not. They're something else. Right?"

"I don't think about them like they're my pets," Elsby mumbled.

"You just seem a little young sometimes. Like, the young kind of twelve."

"Excuse me?" Elsby touched her fingers to her temples in shock. "I'm almost thirteen. My birthday is at the end of August."

Penelope nodded. "I see. Your sun sign is Virgo. Yes, it makes sense, then, why you're so naïve and sweet. See, I'm a Scorpio—the witchy autumnal sign. It's why I'm so talented with everything to do with the occult."

"I'm not naïve. I take the B61 bus alone to my friend Helen's house!"

Penelope shrugged, and Elsby realized she didn't know anything about New York City transit, or how important it was that Elsby's mother let her take a bus by herself, even if it was only for five short stops.

"And I don't care about whatever astrology says, either," muttered Elsby in a very small voice.

"Anyway, I have to get going. I have a lot of other things to do this week, especially if I'm going to work magic with the cats at the solstice." Penelope's face closed up like a curtain was drawn across it. "See you around."

Penelope turned down Pewter Lane without looking back.

CHAPTER FOURTEEN

The Haunted Library

Elsby walked home slowly. She lingered on the front lawn for a minute, trying to look cool as a cucumber, as her language arts teacher Mrs. Parker would often say. She hoped the cats were watching and could see how unfazed she was. So they had given her job to Penelope instead. So what? And Penelope thought she was naïve. *So what?*

Aunt Verity's car was back in the driveway. When Elsby went inside, the house was silent and muggy with heat. In the kitchen, the blueberries were piled up everywhere in bowls and little paper punnets. Elsby tried not to look at them. It hurt to look at them.

She plucked an apple from the fruit bowl and slowly washed it, watching the water run down the drain.

"I like being naïve," she murmured. "And I don't think

the cats are my pets. Penelope is wrong."

She headed upstairs to her own room to think.

When she reached the second-floor landing, she saw that her aunt's bedroom door was open. Bars of golden afternoon light speared through the gaps between the curtains and lit the floor. Aunt Verity stood before what looked like an altar. There was a statue of an angel on it, and some flowers. A thin curl of sweet-smelling incense rose from a brass dish beside it. She was holding a strand of beads and chanting something under her breath.

Elsby took a step toward the attic stairs. A board creaked.

Aunt Verity turned around.

"Elsby, my dear, how long have you been standing there? You look as though you've seen a ghost."

"No, it's not that. I—"

Aunt Verity stepped toward her, clutching her chest. "Oh my goodness. Did something happen to your mother? Did you get some kind of bad news?"

Elsby shook her head. "No, no . . ."

Aunt Verity put a hand on Elsby's shoulder. "I know how hard it must be for you to be apart from your mother."

Elsby's eyes filled with tears. She hadn't been thinking about her mother, not at all. But her aunt's words, and her touch, were like a flashlight suddenly illuminating a dark corner she had been avoiding.

"I know what makes me feel better when I'm glum. Baking! And we have all those blueberries. I'll come downstairs." Aunt Verity smiled.

Elsby tried to smile back, still thinking about the puzzle of what Aunt Verity had been doing, and her worries about her mother. The hallway smelled like incense.

"It'll be fun!" said Aunt Verity.

The truth was, Elsby hated baking. The measuring, the mess, and the way almost anything she made turned out dry as a cracked sidewalk or gloopy as fresh cement. And then all the cleanup. It hardly ever seemed worth it.

The oven itself was terrifying, too. The pilot light in their gas oven back home was always going out. It was Elsby's job to hold down the knob and pray while her mother got on the floor with matches and tried to relight it. Elsby was supposed to visualize it turning on again without them having to call the landlady, but always her most fervent wish was that they wouldn't accidentally blow up the apartment building. Her mother said it was impossible, but Elsby was unconvinced.

Elsby was relieved to find that her aunt's stove was electric, not gas. And that Aunt Verity was content to do all the baking herself, while Elsby sat with a cup of tea and slowly ate the tiny, tart blueberries. Each one exploded on her tongue in a burst of purple juice.

She didn't even have to talk. She just watched as Aunt

Verity rolled pie dough, mixed the filling, and then put the whole thing in the oven. They ate turkey sandwiches while the pie bubbled and hissed behind the oven's glass door.

A thunderstorm rolled in, sending flares of purple lightning through the sky. Then the sun set, and the crickets began singing, and Aunt Verity lit candles, and finally the pie came out of the oven. After it cooled, they dug into their slices. It was wildly sweet and bright.

While they ate, and then cleaned up, Elsby was deep in thought. The cats liked Penelope because she was interested in the same thing they were—magic. Well, Elsby could get interested in that, too. The Athenaeum was right here in Snipatuit. Tomorrow she could go over there and try to sneak into the Room of Enchantment and . . .

Elsby shuddered just thinking about it. Something about that room had felt all wrong. *Dangerous.* But she wanted to seem more knowledgeable. If she did, maybe, just maybe, the cats would like her as much as they liked Penelope.

"We have to make sure these get to Penelope as soon as possible," Aunt Verity said as Elsby washed the dishes in the sink.

Aunt Verity held up a large Tupperware container of blueberries as though she expected Elsby to bring them to Penelope right that minute.

Elsby's stomach twisted around like a trampoline trick. She scrubbed the mixing bowl harder and nodded vaguely. Her aunt put Penelope's blueberries down without saying another word.

The next morning was a bright, fresh Monday. Breakfast was yogurt with blueberries and Earl Grey tea. Elsby ate as fast as possible while the breeze made the curtains dance around her chair. She was relieved when her aunt didn't say anything about delivering blueberries or pie to Penelope. Aunt Verity simply nodded when Elsby announced she was heading over to the Athenaeum to find some more books.

Inside, the library was so dark and damp that it reminded Elsby of that line about Narnia when it was under the enchantment of the White Witch—"always winter, but never Christmas." She shivered as she hurried up the stairs to the second floor. It was hard to imagine that outside it was still a glorious green and gold summer.

She wandered the stacks looking for books on magic. She kept her eyes peeled for Penelope, even though Monday was not her usual volunteer day.

The second floor of the library was deserted. She didn't see Penelope, or anyone else. Yet twice she spun around, sure someone was standing right behind her.

Both times, no one was there.

The Athenaeum was very odd.

Elsby's heart began to pound. She ran her fingers along the spines, reminding herself she was looking for a book on enchanted cats, or really anything that would help her seem smarter to the cats and Penelope. But she struggled to pay attention. Someone was watching her—she was sure of it.

She whirled around again. No one.

She was standing in front of the curling stone staircase that led to the Room of Enchantment. A red velvet rope with a sign that said PRIVATE was strung across it. Something made her want to sneak past it.

"But I can't go breaking the rules," Elsby said, relieved.

She had started to turn back to the stacks when she glimpsed an unearthly pale woman disappearing up the steps.

She leaned over the rope into the stone stairwell. "Hello?"

No one answered.

Elsby wanted to run. Maybe all the way back to Brooklyn. This place was far too creepy.

But another part of her had to know what she had just seen.

She looked over her shoulder, saw no one, and ducked under the rope.

As Elsby climbed the steps, the same uncomfortable,

hazy feeling she'd had when she'd first gone to the Room of Enchantment came over her. When she tugged on the door handle, it creaked open.

Dark, amber light flowed through the windows and lit the seven-sided room. Bronze dust motes swirled in the air.

"Hello?" whispered Elsby. "Anyone here?"

She looked up at the ceiling with its brilliant blue dome and scattering of gold constellations. Then she stared down at the floor, studying the mosaic symbol—that moonish circle with horns and other lines snaking off it.

She stepped into the very center of the symbol. For just a moment her fingers seemed to tingle.

From the corner of her eye, she glimpsed something move. She turned.

A woman stared at Elsby. She had a face Elsby had seen before but couldn't quite place. She flitted in and out of Elsby's vision, like the shadow of leaves blowing in the wind. Her feet were floating a few inches above the ground.

"Elsby!" The ghostly woman reached out her hands. "I must speak with you."

CHAPTER FIFTEEN

The Amulet

Elsby did not wait to hear what else the ghostly woman had to say. She bolted through the door of the Room of Enchantment, down the stairs, and out of the Athenaeum. She ran faster than she ever had before. She sprinted over the streets of Snipatuit all the way to her aunt's house on Silver Crescent.

When she got to the front steps, her heart was pounding. It was sunny and still—a peaceful summer day.

She stared at the cats' side of the house, trying to slow her breathing. And then she realized where she had seen the woman before.

"Rose Fairweather!" she murmured, recalling the photo on the cats' altar.

Could it really have been Rose?

The door opened. Her aunt popped her head out.

"I thought I heard you, Elsby!" Aunt Verity grinned, but her smile quickly morphed into a frown. "My goodness, now you *truly* look like you've seen a ghost. Whatever is the matter, dear?"

Elsby swallowed, unsure what to say.

Aunt Verity hurried down the steps.

"Well, *did* you see a ghost?" she asked, looking Elsby up and down carefully. "Weren't you at the Athenaeum? That place has a rather . . . strange . . . history."

"I—well—maybe," said Elsby.

"I'm listening," said Aunt Verity, carefully folding her hands in front of her.

Elsby hesitated. One part of her wished to tell her aunt everything. Not just about Rose's ghost, but also about the cats, and their enchantment, and Penelope, too.

Another part of her thought it was better to say nothing. Elsby was certain that if she told her aunt about the cats, she would insist on meeting them. And if she met them, what would she do? Take them to her university to be studied? Or, if the cats managed to hide their talents, Aunt Verity could still insist they be sent to an animal shelter.

It was too risky.

"Just . . . some weird shadows in that place," Elsby whispered, looking down at her feet.

"There's been quite a lot of magic performed in that

building over the years," said Aunt Verity. "Some of it has been quite malevolent—evil, really. Perhaps you have a sensitivity to such things. I certainly do."

Elsby looked up. Her aunt's long, narrow face was somber but kind.

"I know something that might help," said Aunt Verity. "Come with me."

Aunt Verity's office was a small room across the hall from her bedroom. It had a paper-cluttered desk with a dusty old computer and many bookcases stuffed with heavy volumes. A threadbare red Persian rug covered the floor and there was a narrow window that looked over the back garden.

From a high shelf Aunt Verity pulled down a dark, polished wooden box. A rich, spicy scent wafted out as she opened it. Nestled inside was a whole gaggle of interesting objects.

There were necklaces with gemstones, and there was a tiny scroll wrapped in golden threads hanging from a string. There was a group of small badges printed with the faces and names of saints, and there was a golden ring engraved with an owl and a crescent moon. There was a hamsa, a small blue hand with an eye in its palm that Elsby recognized from the Middle Eastern groceries and restaurants on Third Avenue back home.

"This is my collection of amulets. Talismans, some of them are also called," said Aunt Verity.

"Like good luck charms?" asked Elsby.

Aunt Verity smiled. "Yes. *Amulet* and *talisman* are just fancier words for that."

"What's that one?" asked Elsby, pointing to a plain gray rock with a hole in the middle. It was strung on a leather cord.

"A hagstone," said Aunt Verity. "People collect them from rocky beaches and other places in England. They're supposed to keep hags—bad witches—and other sorcerers away."

"And that one?" Elsby pointed to a clear, sparkling marble encased in a beautiful net of bronze.

"An Irish charmstone," said Aunt Verity. "Quite lovely, isn't it? Those are dipped in water, and then that water is used to heal animals."

"Oh, I like that. What about that one?" Elsby gestured to a tiny cross made of twigs and bound with red yarn.

"Our Scottish ancestors made these of rowan twigs. There was an old chant that went with them—'Rowantree and red thread/Puts the witches to their speed.'"

Aunt Verity pronounced the words with a Scottish accent. Elsby remembered that it was Aunt Verity's own father—Elsby's great-grandfather—who had been raised on a sheep farm on some windswept island in Scotland's

North Sea before he immigrated to America as an adult. To Elsby his life had always seemed as remote as a fairy tale. But he was her great-aunt's dad.

"People would wear these around their necks or tuck them into their clothes to keep bad witches away. Rowan is a holy plant like that. Very protective."

Elsby nodded.

"You can choose one that speaks to you, to keep as a helpful bit of protection," said Aunt Verity.

"Like, to borrow?" Instantly Elsby worried what would happen if she lost it or damaged it or something. These amulets looked really valuable. Odd, but valuable.

"I have many. Too many for one person. You may keep whichever you choose."

"Keep it? Really?" Elsby's voice squeaked.

Aunt Verity smiled. "Really," she said.

"Thank you," said Elsby.

"Of course." Aunt Verity's face turned serious. "Now, don't go chasing spirits or ghosts or anything else just because you have one of these. You shouldn't be doing any of that sort of thing anyway—no matter what Penelope or anyone else says. There are some nasty things out there, and you must always take care."

Elsby widened her eyes and nodded again.

"A good amulet can help to keep wicked spirits at bay, but it won't save you any more than a life vest would if you decided to jump in the ocean during a category four hurricane," said Aunt Verity.

"Okay," murmured Elsby. "I'll be careful."

"Now, which one calls to you?"

Elsby peered into the box. The Irish charmstone was beautiful—and useful!—but it seemed almost too practical and grown-up. The rowan tree cross was interesting because it was Scottish, like her, but it seemed too plain. Elsby could make one herself if she ever found a rowan tree. Same with the hagstone, if she somehow ended up on a beach in England.

Her eye fell on a tiny glass bottle that hung from a thin gold chain. Its stopper was gold, too; a tarnished and old-looking gold. Something whitish-gray lay inside.

"What's this?" Elsby asked, cautiously picking it up.

"Oh, how interesting that you chose that one. It's a vial of salt blessed by a great saint who lived long ago. That's not glass, by the way—it was carved from crystal. Here, let me help you put it on."

Elsby touched the amulet when it was around her neck. For something so delicate and small, it felt warm and solid.

"Thank you, Aunt Verity," said Elsby.

"Wear it in good health," said Aunt Verity. She closed the box and returned it to the shelf. "Now. I have an errand I'd love for you to run."

"I'll do anything!" Elsby said. "Do you need the dishes washed? Or the bathroom scrubbed?"

"Well, fortunately I had something more fun in mind," said Aunt Verity, laughing. "I have some sweaters that should be cleaned before I put them away for the summer. The Bubble Palace does dry cleaning, too. You can drop them off for me, and bring the blueberries to your friend at the same time. Maybe a few slices of pie as well."

Elsby's heart sank. "My friend?"

"Your friend Penelope?" Aunt Verity looked at her carefully. "Her parents run the Bubble Palace, and I usually see her there in the afternoons when I walk by."

"Oh, right."

Elsby did not want to take anything to the Bubble Palace. Not blueberries. Not pie. Not sweaters. Visiting Penelope was worse than seeing a ghost.

But how could Elsby explain that to her aunt without sharing . . . everything?

"Are you sure you don't want to tell me more about what happened at the Athenaeum?" asked Aunt Verity.

Elsby's aunt was staring at her as though she was waiting for something. She looked ready to hear anything, even something unbelievable, without dismissing it.

But Elsby didn't feel brave enough to tell her.

"No. I'm fine. I'll go right now," said Elsby, swallowing hard.

CHAPTER SIXTEEN

The Bubble Palace

Maybe Penelope wouldn't be there.

That's what Elsby told herself as she followed the map to the Bubble Palace that Aunt Verity had sketched on a piece of scrap paper. It had turned into a humid day, and the air felt sticky as spilled juice.

She walked along Silver Crescent to Pewter Lane, then out to the big road with the cemetery, the bookstore, and Roy's Farm & Food Mart.

When she reached the square where Algernon Endicott's statue loomed, Elsby paused. She stared at the Latin declaration meaning *"I will return"* at his feet, and at his iron boots and his long cloak, and at the crystal ball he gripped in his gnarled hands. Finally she dared to peek up at his baleful face.

His angry eyes seemed to bore directly into her soul. She gasped and ran.

At the corner she checked Aunt Verity's map, then kept walking. On the next block, set back behind a pot-holed parking lot, was a squat brick building. Its sign was hand-painted in white cloud-shaped letters, and in between the words *Bubble* and *Palace* there was a fairy-tale castle made of soapsuds.

Bells chimed as Elsby nudged the door open with her shoulder. The Bubble Palace smelled like detergent, bleach, and dryer sheets, exactly the same as the laundromats in Brooklyn. It was just as noisy, too, with machines clanking and humming under the bright fluorescent lights and ceiling fans whipping the air. A few customers pushed wire carts of laundry around, and others sat slumped in the row of plastic chairs by the door, staring at their phones or books.

The walls were wood paneled. Above the washing machines they were painted to look like stone battlements, and there were faded tourist posters of various European castles above the dryers and folding tables.

At the far back, under a big sign that said "Cashier & Dry Cleaning," Penelope sat alone. Her head was bent low over a book, and her hair covered her face like black velvet drapery.

Elsby raised the Tupperware to hide her own face and

then peered around, looking for Penelope's parents or someone else that she could dump everything with and run.

No such luck.

"Excuse me. I have some dry cleaning to drop off," Elsby said.

Penelope looked up. Her expression rippled from surprised to happy to puzzled.

"Elsby! Fancy running into you here," she said, and smiled. She dropped her voice to a whisper. "I am still in shock. Talking cats!"

"Here are the blueberries and some pie. My aunt made it. Not me. The pie, I mean." Elsby shoved them across the counter.

Penelope looked at the containers, then up at Elsby.

"And my aunt needs these cleaned." Elsby shoved the bag of sweaters across the counter.

Penelope's face flattened. She dropped her gaze and grabbed the bag.

"Is that all?" Her voice was icy.

Elsby nodded, embarrassed. She knew she was being rude, but it felt too late to apologize. Besides, shouldn't Penelope be apologizing to *her*?

Elsby wasn't quite sure. Was it really Penelope's fault if the cats liked her so much? It's not like Penelope could control that.

Elsby passed Aunt Verity's note with her phone number across the desk.

Penelope sorted the sweaters and pinned tags to their labels in silence.

A short little woman, dressed like an old-fashioned doll, emerged from a door behind her. She had black hair like Penelope's, but hers was threaded with strands of silver and gathered in a tight globe on her head. Ribbons, zippers, measuring tape, and cloth were draped over her shoulders.

"My goodness, Penelope! You look like you just ate a sour grape. Try to cheer up for our customers!" The woman had a slight accent, and she spoke around the glittering pins in her mouth. Elsby wondered if she ever accidentally swallowed any of them.

"I'm just doing my job, Mom," Penelope said, not looking up.

"It's okay," Elsby said uncertainly. Why was Penelope so angry?

Penelope's mother glanced from Penelope to Elsby and back again.

Penelope finished labeling the sweaters and pushed the receipt across the table to Elsby. "Ready Wednesday," she said bluntly.

"Penelope!" Penelope's mother spat the pins into her palm. She grabbed the broom that was leaning against the wall and pushed it into Penelope's hands.

"Sweep the front sidewalk," she said sternly. "I'm sorry for my daughter's rudeness," she added, shaking her head at Elsby.

"It's okay. Thank you," said Elsby, and she turned to leave.

When Elsby reached the door, Penelope rushed past her onto the sidewalk.

"I don't smell like dirty socks you know," said Penelope, scraping the ground with a broom.

"What?" said Elsby, bewildered.

Penelope leaned on the broom and squinted at her fiercely. "Just because my parents run a laundromat, and I help out, I'm not dirty. I hardly ever even handle the clothes."

"I didn't say you were dirty!"

"Sure, you didn't *say* it, but clearly you were thinking it." Penelope went back to sweeping furiously.

"Except I wasn't thinking it, either. I wasn't!" Elsby exclaimed.

"Right. Sure. You should know I'm used to it anyway. There's nothing you can think that I haven't heard already from other kids."

"Oh. I—but I'm not like other kids. I swear."

Penelope turned and began sweeping the other direction. Elsby scurried around to face her. Penelope twisted away again.

"That's not why I was . . . I don't care that your parents run a laundromat!"

Penelope stopped sweeping and looked over her shoulder, one eyebrow raised. "Really?"

"Really. I practically live in the laundromat by our apartment back home. My mom and I are there all the time."

Penelope leaned on the broom, frowning. "Then why were you acting so weird?"

"Because I'm jealous," said Elsby in a very tiny voice.

"Jealous of what?" asked Penelope, puzzled.

"Of how much the cats like you," Elsby whispered.

Telling the truth was supposed to make you feel better. But Elsby didn't. She stared at the hot sidewalk, wishing it would crack open and swallow her.

"And because you said I'm naïve, and young," Elsby added in a louder voice. Penelope had been mean to say those things.

"I'm sorry," said Penelope. "I only called you that because I felt wretched right then. You seemed so mad at me, plus I was upset Rose never told me about the cats."

"Oh," said Elsby. Now it was her turn to be surprised. "I'm sorry."

This didn't seem like the time to tell Penelope that Rose's ghost had tried to talk to her at the Athenaeum.

Penelope leaned the broom against the wall. Then she turned and threw her arms around Elsby. "Please don't be jealous," said Penelope. "Don't hate me because the cats like me."

"I won't," Elsby said automatically. "I mean, I don't want to."

The second part was true. Elsby didn't *want* to be jealous. Envy was like getting food poisoning. It felt horrid.

"I'm sorry I called you naïve and young," said Penelope, letting go and stepping back. "And said that stuff about you thinking the cats were pets. I didn't mean it."

"It's okay," said Elsby. Was it? She wasn't sure.

"I just don't understand why Rose never told me about her cats," said Penelope.

"Me neither," said Elsby.

"I thought Rose liked me."

"Maybe she was just nervous? I don't think she told *anyone* about the cats. Anyway, it doesn't matter. The cats seemed to like you right away. Like you're perfect or something. And I'm just whatever. Boring," Elsby said.

"That's not true. You're very interesting. You like to read, and to write, just like them." Penelope paused, as if she was struggling to think of more positive things to say. "They trusted you first."

"But only because I happened to be there," said Elsby miserably.

Penelope bit her lip. "They like you as much as me. I just know it."

It was kind of Penelope to try to make her feel better. But deep down Elsby was sure that's all it was—Penelope being nice. The problem was Penelope had to lie to do it.

"They don't really need me or want me, now that they have you," said Elsby. "It's the truth."

"I won't do anything with the cats without you, okay? Let's swear an oath."

"An oath?" asked Elsby.

"An oath of loyalty."

Penelope shut her eyes, squared her shoulders, and put her hand over her heart.

"Stand up straighter, Elsby," Penelope whispered, after opening one eye briefly.

Elsby hurried to copy her.

"We, Elisabeth MacBride and Penelope Peres, hereby solemnly swear to include each other in anything to do with the cats of Silver Crescent, and not to leave each other out, ever," said Penelope. "May it be so!"

"May it be so," Elsby echoed.

Penelope opened her eyes. She shook Elsby's hand, then grinned. "See, Elsby? Everything is okay now."

"Okay," said Elsby.

"They're just some silly cats. I mean, they're *amazing* cats, don't get me wrong. But they're also silly. So it doesn't matter what they think of either of us. Right? *Right?*"

"Right," said Elsby.

But Elsby couldn't shake the feeling that in agreeing, she was lying, too.

CHAPTER SEVENTEEN

Rough Magic

A week of thick, stormy days passed. Elsby thought the forest around the house could not grow more densely dark and green, but it did. Vines crept up the electric poles and wove shaggy green rugs around the neighborhood fences. Tough little weeds raced over the sidewalk cracks. The green peaches blushed yellow on the tree in the backyard.

Between the spells of rain, Elsby sat in the garden, sketching and writing and looking at the flowers. New ones blossomed every day. In the morning their petals gleamed with dewdrops, and in the afternoons they hummed with bees. Elsby borrowed a plant guide from her aunt and tried to learn their names. Scarlet poppies, plump pink dahlias, bright irises that looked like elegant ladies wearing complicated purple ball gowns. She loved them all, and they took her mind off other, more difficult things. Like the ghost she'd seen at the Athenaeum, and the talking cats, and Penelope.

Elsby tried to be a good friend.

She invited Penelope to go to the ocean with her one morning, but Penelope said she had too much work to do at the Bubble Palace. So while Aunt Verity read a book, Elsby drifted up and down the beach by herself, collecting purple-white quahog shells and pinkish slipper shells, and daydreaming about mermaids and ghost ships. It was a little bit lonely.

It was worse when Elsby asked Penelope to come to Providence, the only big city in Rhode Island. For two days Penelope left Elsby's message unanswered. Then she said she had to finish some summer reading for school instead.

Elsby and Aunt Verity wandered up and down the steep hills full of old wooden houses and around the green lawns of the college where Aunt Verity taught. The city felt haunted, and it seemed like the perfect place to explore with Penelope. But Penelope was more elusive than a ghost.

Elsby suggested that Penelope come over and visit the cats—several times. But she was always too busy.

What was the point of the oath they had sworn if

Penelope didn't actually want to be friends at all?

And why didn't Penelope care about seeing the cats?

Elsby didn't understand it at all.

The cats still had many chores they needed help with, and in the evenings, after Aunt Verity was asleep, they came and got Elsby to do them.

Elsby tightened a leaky faucet. She retrieved a ball of yarn from behind the refrigerator. She opened their cans of tuna.

The cats never mentioned the ceremony nor asked about Penelope. Marzipan was friendly, but not as warm as she had been before. Clarissa was hardly around at all. Elsby glimpsed her just a few times scurrying from her study to the pantry and back again.

Elsby didn't mention having seen Rose's ghost, nor that Rose had tried to talk to her at the Athenaeum. She was afraid the cats would think she was making it up for attention.

The evening after she had gone to Providence with her aunt, Elsby sat in the cats' parlor threading needles. The cats could sew quite well, but coaxing the thread through the itty-bitty metal eyes of the needles was beyond their paws. Marzipan and Tappy sat on either side of her, mending tiny cat dresses and pants and shirts. Horatio was sprawled on the floor, where he was reading out loud from Shakespeare's *The Tempest*.

"'Ye elves of hills, brooks, standing lakes and groves,'" Horatio intoned. "'And ye that on the sands with print-less foot do chase the ebbing Neptune. . . .'"

"Give Elsby that yellow spool next, Tappy," said Marzipan, holding up a small buttercream-colored pinafore that Elsby guessed belonged to Clarissa. "No, the pale sunshine yellow. That one you're holding is more mustard."

"Neither one exactly matches," replied Tappy, sifting through the large tin of threads and buttons.

"Who cares? It's not like anyone sees us anyway," said Marzipan with a sigh.

"Can't you two be quiet?" said Horatio, looking up from the book. His whiskers twitched. "We're getting to one of the best parts, where the magician Prospero talks about how much trouble he's caused with magic and swears to stop practicing it. He's about to break his magic wand and get rid of his book of spells. Pay attention!"

Elsby had been to a performance of *The Tempest* and had a vague idea of what it was about. She knew there was a magician and his daughter marooned on an island, and a kind of ghostly spirit hanging around them, and a strange wild man whom the magician mistreated. Some ships sank. There was enchantment. But she didn't really understand the plot.

Horatio's style of reading wasn't helping, either. He was using a fake British accent, and because Tappy and Marzipan kept chattering, he was practically shouting.

"Honestly, I don't know why we bother mending at all," muttered Marzipan.

"Because Rose always did. She would want—"

"Can't you two *please* be quiet?" cried Horatio.

"Sorry," muttered Tappy.

Horatio cleared his throat and continued.

But this rough magic
I here abjure, and when I have required
Some heavenly music, which even now I do,
To work mine end upon their senses that
This airy charm is for, I'll break my staff,
Bury it certain fathoms in the earth,
And, deeper than did ever plummet sound,
I'll drown my book. . . . .

"Stop!"

Clarissa leaned over the banister, her amber eyes glowing with rage.

"Don't you remember your promise, Horatio?" she continued. "The last time you insisted on reading that stupid play out loud, you swore you'd skip this section. You agreed it was wretched."

"So sorry, Clarissa," said Horatio. He closed the book and cowered, hunching his shoulders as though he was afraid Clarissa would jump down and attack him.

"You're overreacting, Clarissa," said Marzipan, tugging on her thread. "So the magician gets rid of his wand and spell book and quits. Who cares?"

"It's trash," hissed Clarissa. Her ears folded back in rage. "Hardly worth the paper it's printed on. Shakespeare was a—"

Clarissa's eyes fell on Elsby, and she went silent. Slowly her ears rose again. She stared at Elsby intensely—so intensely Elsby began to blush and feel uneasy. She and her aunt had eaten spaghetti with marinara sauce for dinner. Was some still on her chin?

Clarissa swept down the steps and came to stand in front of her.

"Something is different about you, Elisabeth." Clarissa narrowed her eyes, then sniffed.

"We had garlic bread, but I brushed my teeth," said Elsby, covering her mouth.

"Around your neck," said Clarissa, squinting. "What is that?"

Elsby's hand went to the small vial of blessed salt that Aunt Verity had given her. She wore it all the time now, and she had almost forgotten about it.

"It's a necklace, Clarissa," said Marzipan. "Don't you know what a necklace is?"

"Of course I know what a necklace is, dumdum. This

is no ordinary necklace." Clarissa snapped her gaze up to Elsby. "Did a sorcerer give you that?"

"What? No way. I bought it at a tourist shop in New York," Elsby lied.

Elsby stared straight back into Clarissa's eyes. Silence thick as snow filled the room.

Clarissa turned and flounced up the stairs without another word.

After that, Elsby decided to go home. She threaded a few more needles for Marzipan and Tappy, then shuffled across the roof to her room. It was a warm night, but she was trembling. In the distance she thought she heard thunder—or was it in her head? Her heart was pounding so hard she could feel the blood rushing in her ears.

Something was very strange about Clarissa.

Strange—and dangerous.

But what?

After shimmying through her window, Elsby turned on both the lamp next to her bed and the harsh ceiling light. She wished she had candles—she would have lit those, too. Anything to chase away the shadowy dread she felt.

She lay down on the bed and opened a copy of a book called *The Children of Green Knowe* she had found on

Aunt Verity's shelves. It was about a boy who went to visit his great-grandmother at a haunted old castle in England. But Elsby kept reading the same sentence over and over until the words blurred on the page.

Finally she grabbed her phone. It was close to midnight—was that too late to text Penelope?

Oh well.

Elsby tapped out the message with still-trembling fingers.

Something weird happened with Clarissa. Want 2 meet up?

Elsby kept her phone beside her as she slowly put on her nightgown, unbraided her hair, and brushed her teeth. A heavy thunderstorm rolled in. Rain lashed the windows and pounded the roof. The house shuddered like a boat at sea. She tried to read, but she only made it through four pages in an hour. Every other paragraph, she stopped to check her phone.

But there was no reply from Penelope.

Penelope didn't reply the next day, either, or the day after that.

Elsby spent a lot of time thinking about it.

Maybe Penelope had other friends. Ones she liked more than Elsby.

Maybe Penelope had lost interest in the cats, too. No, that couldn't be it. But then—what?

Maybe she was still angry. But then why would Penelope have insisted they swear an oath to never leave each other out? The oath that had been *her* idea.

Maybe Penelope had changed her mind. Maybe she thought Elsby was weird—or worse, *boring*.

That evening Elsby asked Marzipan about it.

It was half past ten, and a warm summer breeze sighed through the screen on Elsby's window. They were sitting on the bed and browsing through a stack of Aunt Verity's books. Elsby had flipped through Homer's *Odyssey*, and some Greek mythology, and then back to *The Children of Green Knowe*. It turned out the ghosts in *Green Knowe* were friendly, which was a reassuring surprise. But Elsby couldn't concentrate.

"You mean why Penelope won't reply to you?" Marzipan looked up from a collection of Japanese ghost stories. She pressed one paw to the lace collar of her dress. "You're asking *me*? For my thoughts?"

"Well . . . yes," said Elsby. "Why not?"

"Because I don't know the first thing about friendship, outside of books. I don't have any friends. Except you."

"What about Tappy?"

"She's my sister. It's not the same."

"Horatio?"

"How can he be a true friend to anyone, when he can't even stand up to Clarissa?"

An uneasy look passed over Marzipan's face as she said this. She peered down into her book. "Oh, wow, this one is called 'The Talking Futon.' A talking bed! How intriguing," she said.

Of course Marzipan would be interested in something that wasn't supposed to talk, but did.

"Um, that sounds . . . fascinating," said Elsby. "But what about Penelope? I can't imagine she just lost interest in *you*. I mean, you and the other cats."

"Uh-oh. Looks like the futon is quite haunted. I'm guessing this story has a really tragic ending," murmured Marzipan.

"Do you think she's just . . . busy?" Elsby continued.

"The futon?"

"No. Penelope!"

"Oh. Probably," said Marzipan, turning the page. "Or maybe her phone is broken. I still find it almost unbelievable that you can just talk to someone far away through a piece of plastic you carry in your pocket."

Cellular phones didn't seem nearly as miraculous as a talking futon or cat—but Elsby decided not to say that to Marzipan.

"Maybe you should go see Penelope in person," said Marzipan, glancing up. "Forget texting. Talk to her face-to-face. Isn't it worth a try?"

"I guess so," The thought made Elsby queasy. "Is she still coming to the enchantment ceremony or whatever on the solstice?" It was only a few days away.

"Oh. I would guess so," said Marzipan, shrugging and quickly looking down at her book again. "But Clarissa is the one handling that."

Elsby touched the smooth little amulet at her throat. She didn't want to ask Marzipan about Clarissa's reaction to it. She wanted to pretend that hadn't happened. Something about Clarissa frightened her.

"I'm planning to skip it, if that's okay," said Elsby. "The enchantment ceremony."

"Good!" said Marzipan. She slammed the book shut and sighed, as if a huge weight had been lifted from her furry shoulders. "I don't actually know what Clarissa has planned." Marzipan looked at Elsby. "If you do see Penelope . . . if you do see her, tell her . . . tell her to be careful."

CHAPTER EIGHTEEN

Sweet Betsy's

The next day, Elsby decided she was done with being ignored. She and Penelope had sworn an oath—and that counted for something. It had to.

It was a Tuesday, and Tuesday was Penelope's volunteer day at the Athenaeum. At half past three, Elsby told her aunt she was heading there to find some books.

The walk to the Athenaeum was long and hot. Vast orchestras of invisible insects were performing symphonies in the trees. Elsby had made the mistake of putting on what she considered her most grown-up and serious-looking dress. But it was long-sleeved and made of burgundy velvet. She could not have picked anything worse.

She plopped down on the Athenaeum steps. There wasn't any sign saying you couldn't. "It's a free country," she muttered under her breath, and scooted into the shade.

Elsby had no desire to go inside even though it was probably cooler—not after her experience with the ghost. She brushed her hand over the amulet on its string around her neck. It was sticky in the heat.

She reached into her tote bag and pulled out her notebook. Scribbling in a notebook was a good way to look busy in public.

The minutes ticked by. Elsby glanced at her tote. It was from the Humane Society and said ADOPT. DON'T SHOP. What would Penelope think of that? Maybe she would take it as a sign of naivete and being too focused on pets. Elsby quickly dumped everything onto the step and turned the bag inside out.

She had just finished tossing her things back in when the door behind her opened.

It was Penelope. Her hair was pulled into a tight bun on top of her head, and she wore a long black dress with a high white collar. She looked like a Victorian ghost, except for her rather normal pair of brown sandals.

She stared at Elsby, and Elsby stared back.

"Hi," Penelope said finally. "What are you doing here?"

"Sitting," said Elsby, scrambling to her feet. "I—I thought maybe your phone wasn't working."

At that exact moment, a loud *ding* came from the black

bag Penelope had slung over one shoulder. She blushed burgundy.

"I've been, um, busy," Penelope murmured.

"Do you want to come see the cats? We could sneak over." Elsby paused, and then took a deep breath. "I'm sure they miss you."

Penelope looked at her. "Do you know Sweet Betsy's?"

"Um . . . no. Is that another Rhode Island ghost or something?"

For the first time, Penelope smiled. "No, silly. It's an ice cream shop. Want to get ice cream?"

Elsby always carried some cash in case she had to take an emergency taxi ride, or buy a bottle of water and a snack from a bodega. Or get an ice cream with someone who might be a friend—or an enemy.

She ordered a plain single scoop in a sugar cone at Sweet Betsy's, which was an old-fashioned little shop with hand-painted signs and overgrown flowerpots outside. They had all the regular flavors, plus a row of "Rhode Island Specials": Rocky Rhode; Coffee Milk; something called the Blizzard of 1978.

Elsby picked mint chocolate chip. She was pleased to see it was a properly fake-looking green color and loaded with chocolate chips.

She worried what Penelope would think—Helen

called it "that toothpaste flavor"—but she decided not to care. And then Penelope surprised her by ordering mint chocolate chip, too.

They took their bright green ice cream outside to sit in some fancy chairs in the shade.

"I like your necklace," Penelope said as soon as they sat down. "Is that salt in there?"

Elsby was so surprised she couldn't speak.

"Did you buy it online or something?" Penelope continued.

Elsby thought of what had happened with Clarissa.

"Sort of," Elsby said, and hoped Penelope wouldn't ask more. Fortunately, she changed the subject.

"I wish I was old enough to start my own ghost-hunting group. Or business." Penelope had finished her ice cream first, and she leaned forward with her elbows on the table and her chin in her hand. "Although I don't even know where to begin with making a logo and everything."

"I could help," said Elsby, though as soon as the words were out of her mouth she cringed.

She remembered Aunt Verity's words of warning when she'd given her the amulet: "Don't go chasing spirits or ghosts or anything else. . . . You shouldn't be doing any of that sort of thing anyway—no matter what Penelope or anyone else says. There are some nasty things out there, and you must always take care."

"You could?" Penelope sat up straight and grinned. "I forgot, you draw! That would be wonderful."

Elsby crunched up the last bits of her cone, wiped her hands, and pulled out her notebook. She pushed away any thoughts of Aunt Verity. After all, it was just for fun. Wasn't it? And maybe this was the way to make sure Penelope didn't ignore her anymore.

"Okay. But no peeking while I work!" she said.

Penelope stared at her phone while Elsby sketched gothic bubble letters that spelled "Ghost Tours of Snipatuit," with two friendly-looking spirits peering from behind the words. Around it all she drew an old-fashioned floral border.

"I love it!" Penelope screeched when Elsby twisted the notebook so she could see it. "Can I keep it? I'll treasure it forever."

"Of course," said Elsby, a happy warmth spreading through her. She pulled the page out of the notebook and passed it to Penelope.

"Maybe I really will be able to talk to ghosts soon and guide other people. . . ." Penelope said, staring down at Elsby's design. "With everything that's happened. Clarissa has been saying—"

"Clarissa?" asked Elsby. Her skin prickled. When did Penelope speak to Clarissa?

Penelope looked past Elsby, as though she was trying to decide whether to share something.

"Well, you see—" Penelope began, then abruptly stopped speaking. She flipped the paper with the ghost tour logo face down on the table.

Elsby turned around.

Two girls in neon tie-dye shorts and white tank tops were standing beside them. One had long brown hair with vivid magenta streaks. The other had lighter hair pulled up in a shaggy ponytail that reminded Elsby of a fire hydrant gushing water. Jumbled rainbows of brightly colored plastic bracelets marched up their wrists. It was like two tropical birds had landed on the sidewalk.

"Hey, Dracula," said the girl with brown and magenta hair, staring at Penelope. She had bright pink braces.

Dracula? Elsby glanced around. Then her heart sank. The girl meant Penelope. And she didn't mean it in a nice way.

"Hi, Willa," Penelope said, glancing at the girl who had spoken. "Hi, Serenity," she continued, nodding to the other one. "This is my new friend Elisabeth. She's from New York." Penelope paused. "New York *City*."

Both girls slid their eyes to study Elsby, who blushed and waved. But neither said hello.

"It's *so* good to see you hanging out with a friend,"

said Willa. She leaned forward and rested a hand on Penelope's shoulder. "A *living* friend. Everyone worries about you, you know? Spending so much time alone. Talking about weird stuff."

"You even found someone who also dresses in dead-person clothes!" said Serenity, scanning Elsby from head to toe.

"It's actually vintage," said Penelope, twisting her shoulder until Willa dropped her hand.

"Vintage? What's that?" said Willa. She raised her eyebrows and looked at Serenity.

"You know the stuff Dracula says never makes sense," said Serenity, shrugging.

Elsby couldn't help it. She giggled. "Why not? Because you flunk all your vocab tests?"

The looks of fake concern vanished from both girls' faces. Serenity made a choking sound and pressed one precisely manicured hand to her chest. Willa curled her lip, flashing hot pink elastic, and stared at Elsby.

"Oh no," Penelope said under her breath, and put her head in her hands.

Elsby's stomach dropped. She'd expected Penelope to laugh, too. But she looked stricken.

"I'm sorry," mumbled Elsby.

Willa glared at Elsby. "When did you move to Snipatuit?"

"I didn't," said Elsby. "I'm just visiting."

"Good," said Willa. "We don't like rude people in this town."

"Have fun picking through the dirty old clothes left behind at Penelope's laundromat while you're here," said Serenity. "That's what you meant by vintage, right?"

"Ew," said Willa. "Come on, Serenity."

Both girls stomped away down the sidewalk, muttering to each other. Twice Willa looked back, scowling.

"They're gone, Penelope," Elsby whispered when they had turned the corner.

Slowly Penelope raised her head from her hands. Her skin was blotchy, and she looked like she might cry.

Elsby's heart was beating very fast. What she'd said to those girls *was* rude—even if well-deserved—and she regretted it.

"I was hoping not to run into them at all this summer," said Penelope.

"They were loathsome," said Elsby, using the biggest word she could think of for *awful*.

But was Penelope going to be mad at how she had talked back to them? After all, Penelope was the one who was going to have to deal with them again in the fall.

"They were in every single one of my classes last year. Willa was my assigned lab partner in science. She liked to ask me questions and then pretend everything I said was ridiculous and incomprehensible." Penelope paused. "She's the one who started calling me Dracula, because I like to wear dark clothes a lot. She said it was 'affectionate,' but . . ."

"It wasn't," said Elsby.

"I know. I guess it could have been worse. Willa and Serenity are not even the meanest kids in my grade," Penelope said, and winced.

Willa's corn-syrupy voice echoed in Elsby's head: *Everyone worries about you, you know? Spending so much time alone.*

No wonder Penelope missed Rose and was so excited to meet the cats. Maybe she didn't have any friends her own age.

But if that was the case . . . why had she been ignoring Elsby?

Penelope picked up Elsby's sketch and stared at it, half smiling.

"Not that those kids matter," Penelope murmured.

"They don't," said Elsby. "They really, really don't."

They talked about thrift stores and clothes as they gathered up their things and headed down Roger Williams Street. The sunlight was turning a deep amber color, and a little breeze that smelled like summer flowers was blowing away the hot afternoon air.

Whatever weirdness had been going on between her and Penelope was over, Elsby was sure. There was no way Penelope would continue ignoring her. Not now.

It wasn't until she was walking down Silver Crescent to Aunt Verity's house that Elsby realized she had forgotten to bring up Clarissa—and Marzipan's warning.

CHAPTER NINETEEN

Nervous Pudding

The summer solstice drew closer, but Elsby didn't get a chance to deliver Marzipan's warning in person to Penelope.

Instead, two days after having ice cream with Penelope, she came down with a stomach virus. Or maybe food poisoning.

Curled up on the bathroom floor, she queasily recalled the shrimp salad the cats had invited her to share. She had been too polite to say no.

There was a knock at the door.

"How are you doing, dear?" Aunt Verity's voice was gentle. "I brought you some Jell-O, if you feel well enough to try it."

Elsby peeled herself off the tiles and limped over to open the door.

"Thank you, Aunt Verity," she croaked.

"Poor thing," said Aunt Verity. "Come back to bed."

Back in Elsby's room, Aunt Verity put the pink Jell-O down on the side table and fluffed Elsby's pillows.

"Are you sure you don't want to be downstairs, Elsby? You could lay on the sofa. I would feel better being able to keep a closer eye on you."

"Er . . . no thanks," said Elsby, crawling into bed. "I'm more comfortable up here."

That wasn't exactly true. Despite the fans, the attic was hot. And lonely. But Elsby wanted to stay in case one of the cats came to see her. They knew she was unwell and had promised to check on her.

And she had questions for them.

Elsby picked up her phone and glanced at it, hoping for another message from Penelope. "I'm so sorry you're sick!!!" Penelope had texted when Elsby told her what was going on.

But when Elsby invited her over to see the cats, Penelope had not replied.

"You remind me of the gelatin," said Aunt Verity.

"What?" Elsby dropped the phone and looked up.

"My mother always called Jell-O 'Nervous Pudding.' Apparently it was nineteen-thirties New York diner slang. Very colorful." Aunt Verity's mouth twitched.

Nervous Pudding? Elsby blinked in confusion, then

stared at the Jell-O. It was still quivering. All of a sudden she got it.

It *was* a nervous sort of dessert. And it was basically a pudding, too.

"Harrowing, isn't it, the trip from the fridge to the plate?" said Aunt Verity. She picked up the dish and handed it to Elsby, then perched on the edge of the bed. "Well, I hope you put the poor nervous pudding out of its misery. Dig in, dear. You need to keep up your strength."

Elsby still had many worries, but they seemed easier to manage as she scooped up the shivering gelatin and let its strawberry sweetness melt in her mouth. She stared out the window. The sun was setting, knitting the sky into a blanket of neon pinks and oranges with threads of lime green.

"I hope it stays clear for the moon tonight. Our ancestors in Britain called the late June moon the Rose Moon—a powerful moon," said Aunt Verity.

"Oh, wow," said Elsby, trying to sound excited. Because it *did* sound interesting.

"May I ask what you might be worried about?" said Aunt Verity. "Besides the dreadful aspects of having a stomach flu."

"Oh. Nothing." Elsby shoveled a large spoonful of gelatin into her mouth.

"All right," said Aunt Verity. She patted Elsby's knee, then stood up and turned toward the door.

"Except—do you happen to have any books on . . . cats?" Elsby paused. "Like . . . magical cats?"

Elsby spent the rest of the evening sitting in bed and browsing the two books of cat folklore Aunt Verity had brought up for her. Both were full of fascinating tidbits. She read about kindhearted, magical Japanese cats who secretly tended fireplaces, and others who were more sinister. She read myths of talking cats in England, and about the Norse goddess Freyja, whose chariot was pulled by cats. Elsby started to feel less queasy, and the hours flew by.

At ten p.m., there was a quick knock at Elsby's window, followed by a hiss.

"It's me," whispered Marzipan. "Can you come? My paws are full."

Elsby put down her book and wrenched open the screen. Marzipan passed her a warm bowl of strange-smelling liquid.

"It's tuna-broccoli-catnip stew," said Marzipan, jumping into the room.

"Wow . . . um, thank you," said Elsby, gagging.

"Tappy made it. I tried to explain to her that humans don't really appreciate catnip flavor but, well, she didn't believe me," said Marzipan, sighing. "Rose was always much too encouraging about Tappy's culinary efforts."

"I'm not sure this will help my upset stomach," said

Elsby, staring bleakly at the smelly grayish-green soup. She held it as far away from herself as possible. "I'm sorry."

"Don't worry about it," said Marzipan. "I'll give it to Horatio. He complains, but really he'll eat anything. How are you feeling? Do you need anything else?"

Marzipan jumped back through the window, and Elsby handed her the bowl.

"Maybe I can scrounge up some other things from the pantry," said Marzipan. "I remember Rose always drank peppermint tea when she had stomachaches."

"That's okay, thanks. My aunt is helping me. But I was wondering—have you heard from Penelope?"

Marzipan's furry face fell.

"I was wondering if she was still coming to the ceremony thing you all are doing on the solstice," Elsby continued. "Since it's only two days away."

"Did you get a chance to talk to her? About what . . ." Marzipan dropped her voice to a whisper. "About what I mentioned?"

"Not exactly," said Elsby.

Marzipan nodded. "I see. Well, I should bring this soup back. I'll come check on you again tomorrow." She scurried along the roof, until her whole face and body fell into the shadows. "And Elsby?"

"Yes?" said Elsby.

"Everything I said about Clarissa..." Marzipan's voice was a faint whisper in the dark. "Well, it applies to you, too. Just be careful, okay? She's more dangerous than you'd think."

After Marzipan left, Elsby stayed up very late reading more about the folklore of magical cats. It was nearly midnight by the time she put on her nightgown and washed her face. She stopped to look out the bathroom window. The moon had risen, huge and pale and round in the sky above the trees. It looked so alive and bright that Elsby half expected a face to emerge and peer down at her. She stared at it in awe.

Something caught her eye. In the greenish-silver garden a small, pale figure swathed in white lace was gliding between the rosebushes. Elsby's breath caught in her throat. She thought of the ghostly woman in the Athenaeum, her hand beckoning—Rose Fairweather not quite dead. She reached for her amulet.

As Elsby watched, she realized that whatever was in the garden was too small to be Rose's ghost. The figure stopped. When it turned and threw back its veil, Elsby saw that it was not a ghost at all.

It was Clarissa.

The cat raised both arms in the air. She gripped a white wand in one paw.

It looked as though light was coming from the tip. It was so faint that at first Elsby thought it was certainly a trick of the moonlight. But as she stared, the glimmer at the end turned into a glow, and then a bright radiance beyond anything natural.

Clarissa froze in place—was she chanting?—and slowly the wand lost its uncanny luster. She lowered the wand, flipped down her veil, and hurried back toward the house.

Elsby's heart pounded. Her queasiness, which had been fading, returned. Whatever Clarissa was doing . . . it was strange. Very strange.

"I have to warn Penelope," Elsby whispered, reaching for her phone.

Hi . . . I just saw Clarissa doing some kind of weird ritual with the moon.
Actually I heard some stuff about her that isn't good. 🙁
R u still going to the ceremony? Maybe don't??
Can we hang out?

A few minutes later, to Elsby's shock, came a reply:

Aren't you sick? 🤭

Elsby quickly wrote back:

Feeling a bit better! Want to meet up tomorrow?? 🍦

There was no answer from Penelope.

Aunt Verity insisted that Elsby spend the following day resting. It was hard. Elsby tried not to dwell on everything worrying her. Curled up in bed, she finished both books on cat folklore and moved on to Egyptian mythology. The Ancient Egyptians *loved* cats.

The book about Egypt inspired Elsby to start writing a new historical novel about a girl who served at the temple of Bastet, the cat-headed goddess, in the time of the pharaohs.

Elsby had written the first two sentences and come up with the title, *The Cat Goddess Girl*. Now she was reading about Bubastis, the ancient center of Bastet's cult, which was near the current Egyptian city of Zagazig.

"Zagazig! That is the most amazing place name I've ever heard," Elsby whispered.

It was such an extraordinary discovery—almost *zigzag*, but not quite—that she shut the book and paced around her room to think about it. Maybe there was a way to bring a modern thread into the story. Maybe it could be a time-travel novel, with one part set in contemporary Zagazig. Yes. Maybe an American girl could go with her archaeologist aunt to Zagazig, and meet a local Egyptian girl, and then discover a portal. Yes! A portal to—

It was when she glanced out the window that she saw it.

A thin figure—much bigger than a cat—in a spruce green cloak with a hood was scurrying across the yard. The person slinked behind a pine and then dashed to the lilac. She looked up toward the house.

It was Penelope.

Elsby's heart lurched. Maybe Penelope had come to see her!

But if that was the case, why was she sneaking around? Why didn't she just text?

While Elsby watched, another figure appeared—a little black cat with no collar, nor any clothes.

Marzipan.

The cat beckoned to Penelope, and the two scurried around the side of the house.

Elsby bolted to the bathroom. She managed to pull up the window that overlooked the garden and stick her head out just in time to see Penelope scrambling through a window on the cats' side of the house, and Marzipan leaping in after her.

Elsby hurried back to her room. She looked at her phone, checking again for a message or call from Penelope.

Nothing.

Well, maybe reception was bad. Maybe Elsby's mother had forgotten to pay the bill, and the line had been suspended, so Penelope's texts hadn't come through. That would explain why she hadn't written back. Maybe—

But wait. If that was the case, why hadn't Penelope rung the doorbell? Or called up to Elsby from the yard?

Why had Penelope worn a cloak with a deep hood to hide her face?

Why hadn't Marzipan or one of the other cats come to tell her that Penelope was visiting?

Elsby slowly sank down on her bed. She felt like she was at the nurse's office in school, trying to hold back the vomit until after her mother arrived and she was safe at home.

Penelope had broken her oath.

And Marzipan had helped her.

Elsby stared at her hands. The bewildered, nauseous feeling flipped over like a pancake. And then, instead of sad and queasy, she was mad.

Spitting mad.

She jumped up and climbed out her window to the roof.

CHAPTER TWENTY

Clarissa's Study

It was easy to break into the cats' house. Elsby tiptoed past the four little beds in their attic room to the hallway, and crept down the first few steps.

Then she stopped and crouched in the shadows.

Penelope was coming up the stairs, Clarissa at her side. The cat wore a pointed wizard hat embroidered with silver moons and stars. A silvery veil was wrapped around her face just below her glowing amber eyes.

Clarissa stopped at the door to her study and reached up for the handle with one paw while beckoning to Penelope with the other.

Penelope pushed back her hood. Her eyes sparkled.

"Is this your study, Clarissa?" she asked.

"Indeed. And I rarely allow anyone to visit," said Clarissa.

Elsby gripped the banister until her palms were slick with sweat.

Marzipan, Tappy, and Horatio appeared on the stairs below.

"Penelope only," said Clarissa, frowning at them.

"But I need to make sure any magic you do is safe," said Marzipan. "I still don't understand exactly what you're planning for tomorrow night."

"Of course it's safe," snapped Clarissa, pushing the door open. "Don't be such a nervous little poodle, Marzipan."

Marzipan let out a small huff.

"Come on, Penelope. Follow me," said Clarissa. "Horatio, keep Marzipan out of my hair!"

"Yes, Clarissa," said Horatio.

Penelope followed Clarissa into the study.

Marzipan stared at the shut door.

"You should really stop making Clarissa mad, Marzipan," said Tappy. "Can't you just go along with her? It makes everything more peaceful. Rose always wished we would all get along."

"We should have told Elsby about this," Marzipan said, ignoring her sister.

"I'll go put on the teakettle," murmured Horatio. "Don't worry so much, Marzipan."

The three cats headed back downstairs, though Marzipan walked very slowly.

As soon as they were out of sight, Elsby rushed down to the landing outside Clarissa's study. For a moment she considered knocking, but she was done being polite.

She wrenched the door open and gasped.

An unearthly green orb floated in the center of the room. Clarissa was perched on a stool. Penelope, eyes glazed over, stood across from her, staring at the glowing light. On a pedestal beside Clarissa was a large, black, leather-bound book open to a page full of odd symbols.

Clarissa glanced up at Elsby, scowled, and swiftly clapped her paws. Instantly the orb of light vanished.

"You rude little grub!" growled Clarissa, glaring at Elsby. "Typical entitled human. Don't you know breaking into someone's home is a crime?"

Penelope looked up, dazed and blinking. Her eyes widened when she saw Elsby.

"I—I can explain, Elsby," said Penelope. "I'm sorry— it's just—"

"It's too late," said Elsby. "You broke your promise."

"What's going on? Elsby, why are you here?" said Marzipan, leaping through the doorway with Tappy and Horatio right behind her.

"That idiot child from next door interrupted my rehearsal," said Clarissa, jabbing her chin in Elsby's direction.

"You *promised*," said Elsby, looking past the cats to

Penelope. "You made me swear an oath that we would always include each other in everything to do with the cats. I believed you. I thought we were friends."

"It's not what it looks like. I really wanted to tell you," said Penelope. "It's just—"

"It's just you *didn't!*" said Elsby. "You're a traitor."

"There are things you don't understand," Penelope said. She pressed her sleeve against her eyes. "Maybe you will at the enchantment ceremony—"

"Ha! As if I have any interest in ever going to any silly ceremonies with you or these cats ever again," Elsby was shouting now.

This was, in fact, a lie. Now that Elsby knew Penelope was leaving her out of things on purpose, she dearly wanted to go.

She turned to Marzipan, who looked down at the floor.

"I'm sorry, Elsby," said Marzipan.

She looked at Tappy, who was staring at Marzipan, and Horatio, whose gaze was fixed on Clarissa.

She glanced at Clarissa, who stared at her with a small, tight-lipped smile.

Tears rushed to Elsby's eyes. She turned and bolted, running down the stairs and out the front door. She clattered down the front steps, not caring if her aunt saw her.

"Wait, Elsby! I can explain!" she heard Penelope yell.

Elsby didn't wait. She ran all the way to the end of Silver Crescent before she slowed to look back, hoping that someone—Marzipan, or Penelope, or even Horatio—had bothered to follow her.

But the street was empty.

CHAPTER TWENTY-ONE

Rose's Book

Elsby kept running. She turned left, then left again. A familiar mottled stone wall appeared. She slowed down and followed it to the bigger road, and then to the main gate of the cemetery. She paused, gasping for breath, and looked in at the huddled gravestones. They seemed sweet and wistful now, not scary.

She kept going past the old Puritan markers with their odd names and short lifespans. Her feet seemed to have their own sense of direction, pulling her beyond Algernon Endicott's mausoleum to Rose Fairweather's grave.

A breeze swirled around her, carrying the scent of flowers.

She quickly looked up, feeling as though someone was watching her.

But only a squirrel, fat and gray as a winter mitten, peered at her from the squat oak tree a few paces away.

Elsby dropped to her knees, clasped her hands together, and closed her eyes. She felt ridiculous. She wasn't exactly sure why she was there or what she was hoping for.

"Please, Rose, if you're out there," Elsby murmured. "Please just help me."

With a prickly feeling, she remembered Aunt Verity's warning about looking for ghosts. *There are some nasty things out there, and you must always take care.*

But Rose was different—she had to be.

Right?

Elsby shivered. It felt as though someone was looking at her again—and not just a squirrel. Could Penelope or the cats have followed her?

Elsby scrambled to her feet. She twirled around.

No one. Even the squirrel had vanished.

Elsby sighed. Why was she disappointed that no one was there? Wasn't she mad at Penelope anyway? She should be. No one had ever betrayed her like this. Not even Helen the time her cool aunt Cindy was in town and Helen picked that girl Tallulah from her tap-dance class to go to the arcade with them instead of Elsby.

"I don't care if I ever see Penelope again," Elsby said. "Or the cats. All of them. And I'm not going to their dumb enchantment ceremony. I'm staying home."

The wind gusted, and the scent of flowers returned, fainter but sweeter.

Gray clouds rolled in and slunk low over Snipatuit as Elsby finally began her trek back to Aunt Verity's house. She didn't *want* to run into Penelope—she'd be happy never to see her again—but she mulled over what she would say to her if she did.

I wasn't looking to make friends here, you know. Cats or humans. I have plenty of interesting friends back in New York City.

This wasn't exactly true. She had Helen. Who couldn't even remember stamps.

But she had the *potential* to make interesting friends at home.

Maybe.

Maybe you read a lot of serious books, Penelope, but I write them.

Or at least, the first chapters.

And I will finish them.

No. This wasn't helping anything. Elsby tried to close her thoughts like you close a browser tab. She plodded down Gold Street, then Pewter Lane, then Silver Crescent. What would she say to the cats if she just happened to run into them, too? *I'm dreadfully busy and it's for the best that Penelope will be helping you instead of me.*

* * *

At bedtime Elsby washed her face, brushed her teeth, and curled up under her cool sheets. She stared at the window, waiting. Surely the cats would come to apologize, or explain, or at least say hello—wouldn't they? Didn't Marzipan care enough to do that?

Finally Elsby stood by the window and looked out.

The night was very black and the waning moon was very white, like one of the marble stones in the new section of the cemetery. Elsby stared at the sky, and the darkness seemed like something alive, something holy, something waiting. But for what?

Dangerous. Horatio and Marzipan had said magic was dangerous, and something about the spell for the cats' enchantment made Elsby uneasy.

But why?

Maybe they meant it was dangerous because of candles or something. Candles could be very dangerous. Elsby often worried about her neighbors leaving candles lit or knocking them over and burning the whole building down.

No. That obviously wasn't it.

She'd seen the green orb in Clarissa's study, and her glowing wand.

"Well, I'm staying home," Elsby muttered, turning away from the window toward her bed. "You all can have some dangerous fun without me."

Elsby switched off the lamp and lay in the darkness, trying not to think too hard about cats, or magic, or friends.

It was a normal dream, cluttered and weird in the way dreams can be.

Elsby found a guinea pig sitting on one of the grimy benches at the West Fourth Street subway station. It was just a regular butterscotch-brown guinea pig, except some of its hair was streaked hot pink. A violin-playing busker on the platform was insisting it was his performing guinea pig, and Elsby needed to pay him fifty dollars to save it from a lonely life of dancing little guinea pig dances for spare change. But she didn't have fifty dollars and she was late for school and had lost sight of her mother. Her dream-teacher was also, horrifyingly, their landlady, and if Elsby was late for school she would increase the rent. The guinea pig stared up at her and squeaked—

"Please listen to me, Elsby, child."

A voice broke through the dream, right into Elsby's mind.

The subway platform melted away, along with the angry violin player and the sad guinea pig and Elsby's fears of the teacher-landlady's wrath.

A woman with long silver hair and a sad, anxious face

stood in front of a wall of books in Clarissa's study.

The same ghostly woman Elsby had seen in the Room of Enchantment.

"Rose!" Elsby murmured.

"Thank goodness you finally called out to me directly. I couldn't break through the wardings put on me until you did, though I tried in the Athenaeum."

"Wardings?" said Elsby, confused.

"Clarissa has put up all kinds of spells to block me from contacting the other cats or anyone else. But she didn't quite figure out how to stop *you*. Especially after you asked me for help. Maybe you have some of your great-aunt Verity's talent."

"My great-aunt . . . what talent?" Elsby asked.

"We haven't much time, Elsby. It takes immense effort for me to speak to you. You must take this and read it." Rose gestured to a small, brown leather-bound book on a shelf. Its spine was embossed with flowers. "Remember where it is. The third shelf from the bottom, between this red one and that thick one with gold lettering."

"But—"

Rose stared at Elsby, her glowing eyes enormous in the dark room.

"I don't have much time. I can only hold off my journey to the next world for a little longer. You must read the book before tomorrow night."

"But—but why?"

"My dear cats are misguided. You must stop the—oh, I can't keep myself together to speak—you must read the book! It will explain—"

As Elsby watched, Rose's body—and the room—began to dissolve.

"Wait!" Elsby cried. She reached for Rose's vanishing arm. But instead she grabbed a fistful of cloth.

Elsby sat bolt upright, the quilt tight in her hand. The little room in her aunt's attic was completely silent, half lit with silvery light from the lingering moon.

CHAPTER TWENTY-TWO

A Bouquet of Roses

The following morning Elsby sat beneath the peach tree in her aunt's backyard. Above her, the yellow fruits hung like round little lanterns from the branches. Her notebook was open on her lap, and her colored pencils were arranged in a tidy line against a tree root.

It was the morning of the summer solstice, and she had a goal: write the first paragraph of the second chapter of *Midnight at the Half-Moon Hotel*, the mystery novel she had begun writing last winter.

Writing stories was the only way she knew how to take her mind off her worries.

Midnight at the Half-Moon Hotel was about a rabbit named Sir Peter Cabbage, who was also a detective. So far in Chapter One she had described the guests at the hotel—mainly other rabbits—and the different ways Sir Peter prepared carrots for his breakfast, lunch, and dinner.

Elsby knew she couldn't spend another chapter discussing food, or introducing new guests with long, elaborate, old-fashioned names, like Amaryllis Ophelia Mesclun-Green. She had to get into the plot. The problem was, she still didn't *have* a plot. She couldn't think of a mystery to solve.

Why did this happen every time?

With her royal purple pencil she doodled petals around "Chapter Two" at the top of the page. But she couldn't focus.

She was dwelling on the strange dream she'd had last night. Never before had she had any dream like it—a dream that didn't feel like a dream at all, but something *real.* It was as if she had been in Clarissa's study, talking with Rose Fairweather.

What did it mean? Did the book Rose wanted her to read have something to do with the cats' ceremony?

Elsby shut her eyes, as if that could blot out the memory of all the things that had gone wrong with Penelope and the cats. The way she had been betrayed. She pressed down hard with her pencil—so hard that it ripped through the paper.

"Argh!" Elsby tore out the ruined page and crumpled

it up. Then she slammed her notebook shut and squinted at the tangled, overgrown garden and the woods beyond.

A small brown rabbit stood by the yellow rosebush, nose twitching. But Elsby didn't even reach for her pencils. What was the point?

"Mysterious, aren't they? Rabbits? They have almost as much magical lore around them as . . . cats."

The rabbit bounded away, and Elsby looked up, startled.

Aunt Verity stood above her. She wore a wide-brimmed straw hat and a small smile, and in her hands was a straw basket with gloves, two pairs of clippers, and twine.

"I'm going to do a little yard maintenance. You're welcome to join me, if you feel up for it."

Elsby jumped to her feet.

They started with a shaggy clump of roses in several shades of sherbet near the cobblestone path.

"Rose Fairweather loved her roses. There are at least three or four individual bushes in this tangle. These darlings need some room to breathe," said Aunt Verity, leaning in with the clippers.

"Do you think the plant minds?" Elsby said, flinching with each snip.

"Oh no. Not these. They wouldn't exist like this without us cultivating and pruning them in the first place.

Roses and people have a long history together." Aunt Verity smiled under her broad hat. "Why don't you put on that smaller pair of gloves and join me? It's quite satisfying."

Elsby followed her aunt's directions, clipping the shriveled blooms and watching for thorns. The scent in the air reminded her of shampoo mixed with cut flowers from the bodega—but fresher and cleaner. Heavenly. It was the same smell that had drifted around Rose's headstone the day before.

"We can snip some of the nice big healthy ones, too. They will make a lovely bouquet for the kitchen table," said Aunt Verity.

Elsby cut several pastel pink blossoms and one that was striped white-and-red like a peppermint stick, and then two small yellow blooms. "Maybe we could bring a bouquet to Rose's grave," she murmured, thinking out loud.

Aunt Verity looked over her shoulder and raised her eyebrows. "What a lovely idea, Elsby. She's buried in the Snipatuit Burial Ground."

"I know," said Elsby. "Penelope showed me."

"Ah, yes. Of course Penelope would have known her, volunteering at the Athenaeum as she does. Penelope seems like such a nice girl."

Elsby focused on a hard-to-reach striped rose the size

of a small pumpkin and nodded, hoping that was enough. Never seeing Penelope again for as long as she lived was fine with her. *Completely* fine. Elsby had her notebook, and she had Helen—sort of. She didn't need more friends.

Especially fake friends. *Traitors.*

But Elsby couldn't shake the ghost she had seen in the Athenaeum—and now the dream about Rose. *Why* was the dream-Rose so worried? What was in the book she was so desperate for Elsby to read?

And what about the other things—the reason Rose had to hurry—what had she said? Something about a journey.

Elsby dropped the striped flower into the basket with the others.

"What would it mean if a ghost talked about trying to hold off their journey to the next world?" Elsby blurted out, suddenly remembering the term Rose had used.

A clump of small yellow blooms tumbled out of her aunt's hand.

"Sorry! Sorry! I'll help." Elsby scooped up the blossoms with shaking hands. Whatever it meant, it seemed to be something that disturbed Aunt Verity.

"Not your fault, dear," Aunt Verity murmured, bending to help her. "But why do you ask?"

Elsby tucked the roses into the basket, taking time to arrange them just so, while not meeting her aunt's eye.

"According to some people, after death—the death of the body—the soul lingers in this world for some amount of time before going on to the next one," Aunt Verity continued.

"How long?" Elsby glanced up and was relieved to see her aunt calmly snipping roses again as if she had never been startled.

"It varies. Sometimes hours, sometimes weeks. Problems arise when you get beyond months. Usually that means the soul has some sort of important unfinished business on Earth."

"But what—"

"This is the sort of thing best left to grown-ups. Were you reading a book in which all of this was mentioned? A ghost story?" Aunt Verity lifted the brim of her sunhat to look directly at Elsby. Her eyes were as bright blue as the ceiling in the Athenaeum's Room of Enchantment.

"No. I . . . I had a dream. It came up in that."

"A dream? Dreams can be quite serious at times."

Elsby had the urge to tell her aunt everything—not just about the dream, but also about the cats, and Penelope and the ceremony, and about Rose appearing in the Athenaeum.

Elsby snipped a few shriveled roses, then chose her words carefully. "Do you . . . do you know a lot about these things? Like . . . death? And magic?" Elsby wasn't sure what exactly you had to learn in order to become an archaeologist.

"I know a little bit. Perhaps more than I should. Magic is quite a dangerous thing to dabble in, you know."

Dangerous. Just like Marzipan had said.

Elsby squatted down. "Well, I mean, I know believing in magic is bad, or at least silly, but—"

"Did I say magic was bad?"

"You said it was . . . dangerous. Isn't that—aren't those the same thing?" Elsby snipped the dead blooms close to the ground and watched as they tumbled into the dirt.

"Are they?"

Elsby scooped up the blossoms and frowned, uncertain.

"When a firefighter goes into a burning building to save someone, that's dangerous, right?" Aunt Verity continued. "But it's also good. It's courageous. Courage can be dangerous."

"That's true."

"And it's safer to say nothing and turn away if you see someone being bullied, is it not? Safer, yes, but is it good?"

"No, it's not exactly good," said Elsby. She snapped the air a few times with the shears.

"Safe *can* be bad, just as dangerous *can* be good. But anyway. Magic. Yes. There is good magic, and there is wicked magic. Wicked magic seeks to harm others, or manipulate them against their will. Wicked magic summons demons, and it uses people. It is *terrible* and must never be practiced." Aunt Verity paused and snipped several dead yellow blossoms. "But, good or bad, courageous or cowardly, magic is never safe. It is dangerous business. Not something to play around with."

Could it be that her aunt actually believed in magic? No—adults didn't. Well, besides Rose Fairweather, and that creepy Algernon person who had founded the Athenaeum. Elsby thought of his statue on Roger Williams Street and his mausoleum in the burial ground and shuddered.

Then again . . . Aunt Verity had those amulets.

"I didn't think magic was real," she said, sliding her eyes toward Aunt Verity.

"Of course it is real," said Aunt Verity, turning to face her. "In fact, it is so real that I rather think there is some kind of enchantment on the modern world making everyone think it isn't." Aunt Verity paused. "Do you mind clipping some more of the ones by the ground, dear? Those ones. Yes, perfect, thank you."

Clip, clip, clip. Elsby stared at the dead flowers, thinking hard about Rose, and the dream, and Penelope, and Clarissa, and the cats. *Clip. Clip. Clip.*

"Well, I think we have enough for several bouquets." Aunt Verity gestured to the overflowing basket. "The roses got a lovely trim as well. I'm sure they are feeling much refreshed. I'll take the clippers and gloves back."

Elsby stood up and handed them over.

"You can always come to me, Elsby, if you have any other strange dreams," said her aunt, stripping off her own gloves. "You know this, yes? I take dreams quite seriously."

Elsby dared to look up into Aunt Verity's eyes. They were serious but kind.

"Let's bring a bouquet to Rose's grave tomorrow. I have some errands and such to run this afternoon." Aunt Verity turned toward the house. "I'll go put these in water."

Elsby drifted back to the peach tree. Its ladder of branches grew up, up, up to the second floor—and the window she was certain belonged to Clarissa's study. It was shut. But was it locked? Elsby squinted but couldn't see from the ground.

Around her, noon heat shimmered above the sunlit patches on the lawn. It was prime time for catnaps.

Elsby hoisted herself up to the first branch. Its bark was gray and shiny, like a satin ribbon, and the tree felt as strong as a jungle gym at the playground. She carefully tested each limb, climbing higher and higher, until she was right outside the window.

The shade was up, and it was not locked. Through the

glass she saw that the study was dark and still, and the door to the hallway was shut.

Balancing carefully, she paused outside the window.

Elsby had only been a tiny bit afraid of climbing the tree. But she was terrified of sneaking into the cats' house. What if they *weren't* asleep? What if they heard her, and confronted her? What would Elsby *say*?

Then she remembered Rose's desperate face in the dream, and what her aunt had said about ghosts who lingered in this world—that they had important unfinished business.

She wrenched the window open and crept in.

Elsby nudged her glasses back up the bridge of her nose and looked around. The room was cold and smelled like a refrigerator in need of a cleaning. But it was exactly as she had seen it in the dream. On one side was the long table cluttered with an hourglass, a crystal ball, jars and bowls, and various stones. Over the table hung that odd sign written in spindly cat's-paw cursive: "To Know, To Will, To Dare, and To Keep Silent."

Opposite it, between the two windows, was the tall bookcase that held the book Rose had beckoned to.

Elsby turned toward the shelves, then hesitated. She peered at the cluttered table. At its center was a cracked black leather tome embossed with silver lettering and symbols. It was the same book Clarissa had been using with Penelope when Elsby had barged in. It seemed like not a book at all, but something alive and slumbering on the table. Like a groundhog or a porcupine or even a small dragon, if books could be like that. But not a friendly sort of animal. A malicious energy flowed from it.

"I should leave well enough alone," murmured Elsby, repeating one of her mother's favorite phrases. It meant "don't invite trouble."

But it was just a book, wasn't it? And books couldn't bite.

She tiptoed across the room . . . and opened the book.

The pages were cold and reptilian in texture, like a snake's smooth underbelly. Elsby flipped around randomly, studying the handwritten, swirling greenish-black ink and symbols. The letters were difficult to decipher.

She paused on a page that was clearer than most and studied the heading.

To Summon a Wraith to Do Your Bidding

Elsby shivered and slammed the book shut.

She turned and looked at the bookcase.

Elsby ran her hand along the many spines, looking—looking—remembering Rose's words: third shelf from the bottom . . . between this red one and that thick one with gold lettering. . . .

With trembling hands she pulled out the book Rose

had showed her—a small leather book the color of milky coffee and tied shut with a leather string. Flowers were embossed on its spine.

Elsby stared at the book, and the window, and then around the study. She imagined Penelope in here, without her, learning from the cats. She wanted to cry.

And then she pictured Rose. Kind, worried Rose.

"Rose? Where are you?" Elsby whispered.

The doorknob turned.

Elsby jumped.

The door opened and a furry black head peered around it. Marzipan.

Elsby pushed the book behind her back and braced for hissing anger.

"Oh, it's you, Elsby! I heard something odd. What are you doing in here? How did you get in?" Marzipan glanced at the open window. "You climbed? I'm impressed!"

"I—I'm leaving now."

Marzipan held up one paw. "Wait. Please. Listen to me, Elsby."

Silent as a mouse, Marzipan shut the door and hurried across the room to Elsby's side. She leaped up onto the windowsill, so she was close to eye level with Elsby.

"Promise me you won't go to the ceremony tonight, Elsby. Please!"

"But why? Why did you pick Penelope instead of me?"

It hurt to say it out loud. But as soon as the words left her mouth, Elsby felt better.

"Well, I'm not really . . . I *do* feel rather bad about Penelope, too. I really do, Elsby. She's probably a nice girl as well." Marzipan closed her eyes and grimaced, then opened them again. "I just know *you* better, and I don't want anything—I just don't trust Clarissa is all. I mean, I don't trust that she knows what she's doing. She *says* that I'm just a worrywart, that everything will be fine, that it won't be dangerous, but . . ."

"But what?"

Marzipan's gaze flicked to the old black book on the table. "She's hoping to perform the ceremony in a new way . . . a way to make the enchantment permanent. Not something that has to be renewed four times a year," she whispered. "And I don't think she's being honest about what it will take to make it work."

Elsby was only half listening. It was hard not to see the truth: Marzipan was coming up with excuses. She and the others preferred Penelope. They thought she was smarter, or braver, or more interesting. Something like that.

"I just wanted to help," Elsby whispered, swallowing the lump in her throat. "And not just with, like, sewing and grocery shopping."

"I think you should warn Penelope not to come," said Marzipan.

"I tried. Penelope doesn't listen to me," said Elsby.

"You don't—oh no." Marzipan's ears suddenly turned toward the door. "Quick! You need to leave!"

A sound of paws skittering came from the hallway, followed by Clarissa's voice hollering. "Marzipan! Marzipan? Where are you? Did you go in my study? You filthy terrier!"

"Go!" whispered Marzipan, hopping down from the sill. "Now, Elsby!"

Still clutching Rose's book, Elsby scrambled out the window and into the tree.

It wasn't until she was all the way down on the ground again that she realized she hadn't told Marzipan about the dream.

CHAPTER TWENTY-THREE

The Diary

Elsby hurried up the stairs clutching her notebook and pencils in one hand and Rose's book in the other.

When she reached her room, she threw herself down on the bed, unwound the string around the book, and began to flip through the pages.

She was surprised to discover it was a diary, one not so different from her own. There were doodles in the corners, and sketches of flowers and cats. The entries were from the past few years, all written in a beautiful cursive that flowed across the pages.

Elsby paused to read a random paragraph. Disappointingly, it turned out to be a lament about library budgets and malware in a new catalog software system.

"Oh. This is *your* diary, Rose," Elsby murmured.

"Elsby! Elsby?"

Startled, Elsby slammed the book shut.

Aunt Verity stood in the doorway. "I've been calling you for a few minutes. Everything okay?"

"Um, yes. Just distracted. Sorry."

"It's all right. Come on down. It's lunchtime."

Elsby ate lunch quickly, then hurried back upstairs to keep reading. At dinner she raced through Aunt Verity's fire-truck red spaghetti puttanesca and washed the dishes at warp speed.

A few times she noticed Aunt Verity peering at her as if she knew something was up. But luckily her aunt didn't ask any questions.

After cleanup was done, Elsby turned down Aunt Verity's offer to play Monopoly. "I didn't meet my word count goal for the day," she said, which was true, but also a fib, because she had no intention of working on any of her novels.

She had to get back to Rose's diary, even though it was pretty dull. Rose wrote a lot about her problems at the library—and sometimes about the garden, which was suffering an aphid infestation which no amount of homemade peppermint oil spray would fix. It turned out Rose had also liked watching the bunnies and had often sketched them.

There were drawings of the cats, too, but fewer notes on them than Elsby expected. Was Rose worried they would read the diary? It was left on a shelf in Clarissa's study, after all.

Elsby began to wonder what exactly Rose had been so eager for her to find in the diary. Were the garden descriptions written in some kind of secret code?

The sun set, the moon rose, and Elsby grew more bewildered.

But then, just after ten p.m., she read something that felt like a clue. It was from the previous summer solstice exactly one year ago.

Tonight I renew the enchantment, holding my breath that the previous effects don't recur . . . but I fear the years of spellwork for my dear cats may have caught up with me at last.

Two days later, Rose wrote:

It is even worse than before. I have laid in bed ever since the last ceremony. My heart struggles with each beat. I feel the life force ebbing from me like an ocean tide receding from the shore. Will it ever return? Perhaps my body is now a cracked bowl, slowly leaking out my energy and soul.

My poor, dear cats. I would do anything for them. I would suffer anything for them.

That didn't sound very good. At all.

Elsby began reading faster, skimming the sections about plants and wildlife and Rose's job at the library.

Just after the autumn equinox came another entry.

Again I have done the spell, and my sweet cats continue to live and to speak. But the years catch up with me. It's clear now how periods of weakness follow each new round of enchantment. What shall I do?

I have been trying to get my affairs in order and prepare supplies for the cats, for I know my time is short. But whom can I trust? Not Ashley nor Tiffany . . . yet I have no others. Perhaps my neighbor Verity is trustworthy—she has a certain mystical quality, a sense of mystery and integrity and spiritual depth—but I fear the consequences if I'm wrong. So I dare not say a word.

I have told the cats, if the worst comes and they are in dire straits, to ask a child for help. . . . A child would be less likely to exploit them if they revealed the truth. I hope the spellwork holds.

I fear the future.

"This sounds terrible," Elsby murmured.

She glanced at the time. It was almost eleven.

She skipped ahead to an entry after the most recent winter solstice.

I have told the cats they must under no circumstances follow Clarissa's plan. Better they should pass into the next world than harm an innocent person and carry such a stain on their souls.

"Uh-oh," Elsby whispered.

Just what was Clarissa planning?

No wonder Marzipan had seemed so worried!

Elsby flipped through the pages faster and faster. Just after the spring equinox came the most troubling entry yet.

The end draws near. There seems to be no repairing the damage already done, so I performed the spell one last time in the hope it would help them for a little while after I am gone. My dear cats speak and live, but at great cost to me. My body has been drained of all vitality. Yet I would do it all again for them, the ones I have loved most in this life besides my dear husband. And I have loved them all so deeply—even Clarissa, troubled though she is.

I worry that once I am in the next world, Clarissa will persuade the others to try that dark spell she discovered in an old grimoire of Algernon's, in the darkest reaches of his dangerous room—a spell to steal a human soul to fuel the enchantment forever. And worse . . . to call up the dead to help. . . .

It must never come to pass! It is evil. I fear it will kill outright whomever Clarissa attempts to ensnare. Yes, it may grant her and other cats eternal life, but at what cost? Murder! Clarissa assures me she won't try it—but I do not trust her.

Elsby turned the page. But the next one, and all the ones that followed, were blank.

"Penelope," she whispered. "Penelope!"

She shut the book, leaped off the bed, and checked her phone. It was already half past eleven. There was hardly any time.

For a brief, cowardly moment, Elsby stared at the phone, and at Rose's diary, and then at her bed.

She thought about what Rose had said in the dream, and saw her wavering, worried face, kind and scared, staring at her, pleading. *Stop them.*

No one but Rose's ghost knew that Elsby knew the truth. Elsby could stay safe and snug in her room, leaving Penelope to her fate. What did she owe Penelope, anyway? She was rude, and bossy, and talked too much, and she was so sure she could handle anything. Above all, Penelope had betrayed her.

But then she thought of Penelope's mother, worried and kind, and her own mother. What would Elsby's mom do if something ever happened to *her*? She wouldn't be able to go on. Was it any different for Penelope's parents?

What if Penelope *couldn't* figure this one out on her own?

Rose's ghost certainly thought she was in danger.

"I have to stop this," Elsby said.

With trembling hands, she picked up her phone and called Penelope. Twice the call went straight to voice mail.

You're in danger!! Don't go to the ceremony! Elsby texted. But what if Penelope didn't see the message?

Elsby felt for the amulet around her neck. It was warm and solid in her hand. It had scared Clarissa. Would it be enough?

"I have to try," Elsby murmured.

She grabbed one of her tote bags and tossed in the flashlight and her phone. She jammed her feet into her sandals, before thinking better of it. She slipped them off and held them by the straps as she tiptoed down the stairs.

On the second floor, in the gloomy shadows, she hesitated outside her aunt's door.

Knock, whispered a small voice inside her head. *Tell her. Rose almost did.*

Elsby raised her hand.

She remembered her aunt's words in the garden: *"You can always come to me, Elsby, if you have any other strange dreams."*

But this wasn't a dream. And what if Aunt Verity didn't believe her? What if she stopped her from going to the Athenaeum? There wasn't much time, and if what Rose wrote was true, Penelope's life was at risk.

Elsby let her arm drop. She crept down the stairs and into the dark silence of the night.

CHAPTER TWENTY-FOUR

The Room of Enchantment

The darkness was thick and still. Up in the sky the constellations prickled with silvery light.

Elsby sprinted down Silver Crescent and on to Roger Williams Street, the amulet bouncing against her throat. She passed the graveyard, the shops, and the Bubble Palace, then turned again, toward the Athenaeum.

Moonlight wrapped its turrets in iridescent light. The windows were dark, blank eyes, except for those in the tallest tower, which glowed yellow.

"The Room of Enchantment," Elsby whispered.

Elsby hurried up to the double doors. The cats had a key, and she hoped that they hadn't locked the doors behind them.

She tugged on the cold iron loops and exhaled with relief when the doors creaked open.

Elsby switched on her flashlight, holding it steady with both trembling hands.

The beam swept across the slumbering computers, the tall plants, and the empty tables. She tried not to think about what might be lurking in the vast darkness beyond the flashlight's yellow glow.

She swung the light toward the stairs, sweeping over the knight's armor. Then she started to climb to the second floor.

At the top of the steps, she hesitated.

A soft yet insistent current, like the kind you feel when you wade into the ocean, tugged at her.

It pulled her through the long stacks to the left, then doubled around behind the history section. It became stronger, and there they were: the stone stairs whorling up the tower to the Room of Enchantment.

Elsby climbed the first step.

Like the inside of a seashell, the stairs were whispering with echoes. Someone was chanting.

She felt the pull again, now strong as a rip current those signs at the beach warned you about. She zoomed up the rest of the steps.

The door at the top stood open, and the room beyond blazed with candlelight.

Elsby stepped in and the door slammed shut behind her.

Penelope stood in the middle, in the very center of the circular black and white mosaic symbol on the floor. She wore a black lace dress with a wide collar and old-fashioned black patent leather shoes. Her expression was curiously dazed—just as it had been when Elsby had barged into Clarissa's study.

Three cats stood around her. Horatio was on the right, and Marzipan and Tappy on the left. They were dressed in simple white shifts.

Clarissa perched on a stool beside a table draped in purple cloth. On it were a bell, the big black book, and a candle. She wore black velvet robes and a mage's pointed black velvet hat, stitched with silver stars. Her ears poked through two holes. In her left paw was a small ivory wand—the same wand Elsby had seen her use in the yard.

Clarissa chanted in a low, purring tone. Her gaze flicked over to Elsby, then back to Penelope.

The other cats turned.

"Elsby! What are you doing here!" cried Marzipan, paws on her cheeks. "I tried to warn Pen—"

"Hush!" hissed Tappy. "You're going to make Clarissa mad."

A look of worry passed across Penelope's face, but she didn't move.

Clarissa chanted louder. The uncanny current that had tugged Elsby up the stairs seemed to be coming from her wand and her words.

"Stop!" cried Elsby. "I know what you're doing! I know what this did to Rose. You have to stop, Clarissa!" She tried to run toward her, but Clarissa waved her wand, and suddenly it was as though Elsby was wading through thick honey.

"Stay out of it, Elsby—Clarissa is helping us!" said Horatio.

The vial of blessed salt around Elsby's neck tingled. She lifted it and stared at Clarissa. The cat glanced at her, and then at the amulet, and seemed to cringe.

"Helping *who?*" Elsby struggled to take one step after another, inching closer. "These rituals gave you the power to talk and live and so much more, but they slowly *killed* Rose! And now you want to sacrifice Penelope. But I won't let you!"

Marzipan looked at the others. "I told you we couldn't trust Clarissa, but—"

"Shut her up, Horatio," snapped Clarissa.

"Quiet, Marzipan!" Horatio grabbed Marzipan.

"Don't hurt my sister!" yelped Tappy, running circles around them.

Elsby took another staggering step forward. She reached up. Clarissa's swishing tail was just—almost—there. She grabbed it and yanked.

Clarissa screeched.

An electric jolt hit Elsby and she let go, stumbling onto the ground.

"Elsby! Are you all right, Elsby?" cried Marzipan.

Pain shot through Elsby's arm all the way to her heart. She gasped, unable to speak.

Clarissa whisked her wand lightly, as though she was shaking some mud off of it. She gave Elsby a malevolent look.

"There's more of that coming if you try anything again, Elisabeth," Clarissa said. "Not that you can do much. Penelope agreed, and the enchantment is almost complete. And your pesky little amulet won't save her, or you."

Penelope, in the center of the mosaic, remained still and silent as a doll.

"You tricked her. She didn't know what she was agreeing to!" Elsby cradled her elbow and inched across the floor, dragging herself on her good arm. The amulet dangled from her throat and sparkled in the candlelight.

"Ah, perhaps." Clarissa smiled. "But Penelope should have known magic is something one must study for years and years, for lifetimes, really, to have any effect. But you humans are so stupid and full of yourselves! How easy it is to confuse creatures who *care* so much!" Clarissa laughed. "Well, now you'll see."

"You don't speak for all of us cats," said Marzipan, struggling against Horatio's grip.

"You're wrong, Clarissa," cried Elsby. "You know you're wrong!"

Clarissa twirled her wand. She ignored Elsby and grinned at Marzipan. "Oh, you're just as bad, Marzipan. You *wanted* to think what I was doing wouldn't hurt anyone. Because you long to stay alive, speaking and reading and everything else. Deep down you knew the truth, and you let me lie about it."

Marzipan's eyes slowly filled with tears.

"Your problem is you are too soft about humans, Marzipan. Frankly it's a small price to pay, no? A bargain. Penelope was just one girl, and we are four cats."

Was. Past tense. How far had Clarissa's spell gone? What if Elsby was too late!

"Evil! Rose worried you were evil, and she was right. She should have dropped you off at the animal shelter!" cried Marzipan. She tried to shrug Horatio's paws off her shoulders.

"Marzipan, please, please, please be careful," whispered Tappy.

"Clarissa is right, Marzipan," said Horatio. "Stop resisting! Just listen to her."

"The humans have you brainwashed, Marzipan," said Clarissa. "Think about everything humans have done to cats in history. To all animals. To *you*. What do we owe them?"

"There are millions of people like me and Rose—and Penelope—who care for animals, Clarissa," Elsby said, still dragging herself forward inch by inch. "Besides, don't cats kill birds? Mice? None of us is really innocent."

"I really don't understand you, Elisabeth." Clarissa sighed, shaking her head. "You say you care about us. So why are you trying to stop me from the one thing that will ensure all of us—Marzipan, too—live?"

"Because—because it will hurt Penelope!"

"The spell is already in progress and I'm beginning to be annoyed with your antics. Now then." Clarissa raised the wand and began to chant.

The pain seared through her arm, but Elsby didn't care. She took a deep breath and flung herself forward, knocking Penelope to the ground. Penelope's glasses fell off.

"Wake up!" Elsby shrieked, grabbing Penelope around the waist. "Wake up!"

"Bothersome, bothersome." Clarissa scowled, pointing her wand directly at Elsby. "Or maybe an unexpected boon. Let's see if we can double the magic. My helpers from the other realms will have to work hard for me tonight."

She began chanting again.

And then Elsby felt it: a great pressure, like something was being pulled from her heart. She gasped as a rosy-gold glow began to emerge from her chest. The same thing was happening to Penelope on the ground beside her. The glow swirled into two ribbons of mist and zipped toward Clarissa.

"Mar-mar-zipan! W-w-what's happening?" Elsby cried, forcing the words out. She let go of Penelope and tried to stand, but her knees buckled. She gripped the amulet with shaking hands, trying to wrench off the stopper. Maybe, just maybe, there was a way to stop Clarissa.

"She's trying to take your life force!" Marzipan screeched. "Clarissa, stop! Horatio, let go of me, you traitor."

Marzipan bit down on Horatio's paw. He jumped back, hissing, and Marzipan catapulted onto Clarissa's table, yowling. Tappy jumped back and screamed.

Clarissa, still chanting, leaped over Marzipan and landed on the floor. She turned and flicked the wand once in Marzipan's direction.

Marzipan slumped over on the table, her eyes shut.

"No! No!" bawled Tappy, running to cradle her sister's motionless body.

Clarissa turned again, a grin on her face. A tendril of green smoke grew from the end of the wand. It slithered across the room like a snake, and when it met the golden-pink mist, it flared bright purple with a jolt that shook Elsby to her core. She let go of the amulet. Its stopper was still stuck fast.

Elsby sank to the floor in a heap. Her bones felt like jelly. She felt herself fading, fading, fading. The mist was all green now, a dark, swampy green that clung to her whole body.

As Elsby gazed through the fog, a form began to take shape on the floor near Clarissa. It was hazy, and silvery, and tall. And familiar.

It was Algernon Endicott.

His fierce gaze was unmistakable. He looked just like his statue—just as cruel.

But he was no statue now.

He spun around the room, glaring from the cats to Elsby and Penelope.

"It's me you're looking for. Welcome, Arch-wizard," said Clarissa. She bowed slightly. "Tonight I have *two* living souls for you to take, not one. A gift in exchange for assisting me in giving us our eternity. These two."

Clarissa gestured to Penelope and Elsby, and Algernon glowered down at them.

Elsby managed to raise her hands to the amulet and grip it again. "Use every last itty bit of your strength," she said to herself. She tugged hard. Her hands were sweaty now, and it slipped. She tried again.

"I must warn you, Arch-wizard, that the mousy-looking one has a powerful amulet around her neck," said Clarissa. "We'll first have to break its power with a special—"

Pop.

The stopper came free. Elsby held the tiny crystal vial in her hand. She managed to raise herself to her knees. She couldn't speak, nor walk, but she could still throw. With the amulet gripped tight in her fingers, she lifted her arm and pitched the salt in Clarissa's direction.

"Ahhhh!" the cat screamed, and cowered.

There was a bang, and then a muffled cry. Elsby looked behind her. In the murk she saw a thin figure.

Aunt Verity?

Aunt Verity was chanting in a language Elsby didn't recognize. She stepped in front of Clarissa and raised her hands.

"No!" roared Clarissa.

Bright light beamed from Aunt Verity's palms toward Algernon, who opened his mouth in a silent scream. His wavering form steamed and dissolved. A moment later he was gone.

A feeling like soft spring sunshine wrapped itself around Elsby as the sludgy green mist vanished.

"What's happening? What's going on? Why are we on the ground?" Penelope gazed at Elsby.

"Clarissa tried to kill us," said Elsby, trying to stand up. She gripped the empty vial in her palm. Everything hurt. "And I don't know if she's done yet."

Clarissa let out a long hiss.

"Stop! I command you to leave these children unharmed," cried Aunt Verity. Her hands still raised, she glared at Clarissa, who stood on the table, one paw on the slumped pile of black fur and white cloth that was Marzipan. Tappy huddled beside her, sobbing.

Clarissa glared back. Her hiss grew louder.

Aunt Verity took a step forward. "Be gone. Scat!" Her voice echoed around the tower room. The candles flickered.

Clarissa shrieked. Then she tugged off her hat and her robes, chomped her wand between her fangs, and on all fours dashed toward the stairs.

"Wow," Penelope said in a dazed tone.

Tappy pulled Marzipan's limp body into her arms. "Somebody help my sister," Tappy wailed.

Elsby looked at Marzipan and felt her own tears begin to gather. "No. No, no, no. Please wake up, Marzipan. Please!" She stumbled to her feet and rushed to Marzipan's side.

"She's still breathing," whispered Tappy.

"Wake up, Marzipan. Wake up!" Elsby cried.

Aunt Verity and Penelope came to stand beside her.

From the corner of her eye, Elsby saw Horatio hiding behind a chair with a worried look on his face.

"Come on, Marzipan," Elsby whispered. "You have so many poetry books still to read. So many poems to write. Breathe!"

But even as she said it, Elsby wondered if Marzipan would still be able to read, or speak, if she lived.

"Breathe, Marzipan, breathe!" Penelope said hoarsely.

Marzipan took a staggered breath and slowly opened her eyes. She focused her gaze on Elsby. "Elsby . . . Penelope . . . I'm so sorry. I hope you can forgive us," she said.

"It wasn't *you*, was it?" said Elsby. "It was all Clarissa."

"And Horatio," said Marzipan.

Elsby turned around slowly and then took a few quick steps to the left.

"Got you!" she said, lifting Horatio by the back of his white tunic.

Horatio cowered, covering his eyes with his paws.

"You were ready to sacrifice Penelope and me, weren't you? And let Clarissa do whatever to Marzipan? Talk about ungrateful!" Elsby shook him furiously.

"Elsby, I'm sorry! I really am!" Horatio whimpered. "I was afraid of her."

"Yeah, right, like I really believe that." Elsby hoisted Horatio higher.

"It's true he's terrified of Clarissa," said Marzipan with a sigh. "Horatio has about as much backbone as an unbaked baguette, and she's bullied him for years."

"It's true. I'm a coward! Forgive me," said Horatio.

"Elsby, let him go for now." Aunt Verity put a hand on Elsby's shoulder. "We'll deal with him later."

Elsby dropped Horatio. He coughed and scampered under a table.

"Neither he nor that other one can hurt you now," said Aunt Verity. She looked at Penelope. "But why are you both here? Why did you ever think it was a good idea to come? And what—or *who*—are these cats?"

Elsby glanced at Penelope, who still looked stunned. Then she stared down at the floor, and whispered, "I'm sorry, Aunt Verity. I really am. I know we shouldn't have come here alone."

"But why did you?" asked her aunt.

Slowly, flinching slightly, Elsby raised her eyes.

She saw that Aunt Verity was not angry. She seemed . . . curious. And kind.

"It's . . . you see. Well. The cats—and Rose—" Elsby took a deep breath. "Rose Fairweather came to warn me about what Clarissa—that's the evil cat—was going to do. In a dream, I mean. She led me to her diary where I read . . . well . . . a warning. These are *her* cats, you see. She enchanted them long ago so they would be able to speak and read and be like people. They've actually been in her house the whole time. Penelope and I—well, we thought we were helping them. The cats, I mean."

Aunt Verity nodded, slowly and surely, as if all of this was completely and easily believable.

"Why didn't you come tell me, Elsby?" she asked.

"I was afraid you would think I was . . . making it all up," said Elsby. But no, that wasn't quite true. Elsby paused. "I mean, I was afraid you would stop me somehow from visiting them. Or . . . I don't know. I was just afraid."

Aunt Verity nodded again. "It wasn't a good choice, but I can see how that would happen."

"But how did you know where we were?" asked Elsby, holding back tears of relief.

"I had the strongest, most unshakable urge to get up and check on you in your little attic room. When you weren't there, I thought back to our conversations, and a single word echoed in my head: *Athenaeum*. So I hurried over here."

"Thank you," croaked Penelope, her voice cracking.

"And thank you for the amulet," said Elsby, tightening her fist around it. "I think it really helped me."

"We must make haste," said Aunt Verity. "We aren't supposed to be in here. Cats, girls, let's put out these candles."

"Verity, can I ask you a question?" Penelope asked, her voice almost back to normal. "What did you do and how did you know how to do it?"

The room was swiftly darkening. Aunt Verity puffed out three candles in a row, then spoke.

"That is a very good question with a very long answer," she said, stepping between the shadows. "All you need to know for now is that I sent that dreadful shade Algernon Endicott back where he belongs. Then I deflected the soul-stealing spell before that cat sorceress—Clarissa, is she called?—could finish sucking the life forces from you girls. Instead it went through me and did not harm you." She paused. "I hope."

"I don't feel harmed," said Elsby.

"Me neither," said Penelope, adjusting her glasses.

"And we can still speak," said Marzipan.

"Are you okay, though?" asked Elsby, studying Aunt Verity in the dim light.

"The spell took some of my life force," said Aunt Verity.

Elsby gasped. "But—"

"Help me blow out candles," Aunt Verity said. "Someone in town might see the light and come investigate, which would make this evening even more difficult than it already is."

"Took some of your life force . . . does that mean—is your life going to be shortened, like Rose's was?" Elsby looked at her aunt, and her heart sank. "I think that's why she died. From these spells she did for the cats."

"Don't fret, my dear. I should be fine. Magic is dangerous business, and I'm not sure Rose really knew what she was doing. But fortunately, I do. Now, I'm going to blow out this last candle. Then follow me down the stairs. I'll turn on the flashlight when we're away from the windows."

The last flame snuffed out with a hiss. The Room of Enchantment was pitch-black and spicy with the scent of beeswax and burnt wick, and the deeper layer of frayed magic.

"But Aunt Verity . . . what if you hadn't come? What would have happened to us? Would we have . . ." Elsby couldn't bring herself to finish her sentence.

There was a long pause, then her aunt's voice came up through the darkness, warm and mysterious. "It was rather perilous, wasn't it? But I believe you had already found a way. You are stronger than you know."

CHAPTER TWENTY-FIVE

Mint Chocolate Chip vs. Coffee Ice Cream

Rose Fairweather's pink quartz headstone glistened in the downpour. Shivering in her damp dress, Elsby gripped her borrowed umbrella tightly in one hand and the bouquet of roses more loosely in the other, taking care to avoid the thorns.

"There! I just managed to get it to light. Oh, please don't go out, little candle," said Penelope, standing up and grabbing her own umbrella back from Aunt Verity.

"I'll try to shield it," whispered Marzipan, curling up near the glass votive on the grass, blocking it with her paws. "I do wish I had my dress and wool cape. Or even just a bonnet!"

Horatio peeked from behind the stone. He truly could not stand being naked, and he still seemed embarrassed that he had sided with Clarissa. *As you should be*, thought Elsby, glowering down at him. She wasn't sure she would ever be able to forgive him, no matter how many more times he apologized.

Tappy hugged the gravestone, weeping less than Elsby had expected. In fact, she looked almost content. "I'm just so relieved that Rose appeared to you, Elsby," she murmured. "I always knew she was watching over us. Do you think she'll finally come back to speak with us, since Clarissa ran away and her horrible spells seem broken?"

"I don't think so, dear," Aunt Verity said gently. "Now that her mission here is complete, I believe Rose has fully passed on to the next world."

Tappy let out a soft sob and rested her head on the grave. Marzipan gently patted her shoulder.

"Thank you, Elsby," murmured Marzipan, looking up at her. "Without you and your aunt, I don't know what would have happened to us."

"Or me," Penelope whispered, glancing Elsby's way.

Elsby quickly tilted her umbrella so she didn't have to look at Penelope. She was glad Penelope wasn't dead—but she was mad. *Really* mad. Penelope still hadn't apologized, or even attempted to explain why she had broken their oath and betrayed her.

"Why don't you say a little prayer, Penelope," suggested Aunt Verity.

"All right." Penelope's voice was shaky, and dark circles shadowed her eyes. She was clearly still weak from her ordeal the night before, but she put down her umbrella and stepped forward. She extended her arms, palms up. The rain drizzled down on her.

"Dear Rose, thank you for helping us. We hope you are at peace. We will forever be grateful to you. May your soul be blessed now and always." Penelope brought her hands together and slowly bowed.

"Amen," said everyone in chorus, though the word caught in Elsby's throat. She wanted to cry.

"Elsby, will you place the bouquet?" asked Aunt Verity.

Elsby stepped forward, her feet squishing the damp grass, and lay the bunch of roses against the headstone. In the rain they were bright and luminous as candy. It seemed far longer than yesterday since she had stood talking in the garden with her aunt as they snipped them.

"Be well on your journey, Rose," Elsby whispered. "And thank you."

As they trudged back through the cemetery toward the car, Elsby tried to keep two steps ahead of Penelope. She wove around out-of-the-way headstones and half ran on the slick grass until she was far in front of everyone.

"Wait, Elsby!" Penelope called out, just as Elsby reached the gates.

Penelope had closed her umbrella and was jogging toward her with wide, beseeching eyes. Behind, Aunt Verity and the cats were coming down the hill. Tappy was riding on Aunt Verity's shoulder.

Elsby stopped. She clenched her umbrella handle so hard her palms hurt.

Rain plastered Penelope's hair to her forehead. Her long black lace dress—the same dress she had worn the first day they met in the library—was soaked and dripping water.

"I'm sorry." Penelope rested her hand on her heart. "I'm so sorry. Truly, deeply, sorry. Can you ever forgive me for betraying you?"

"I don't know," said Elsby, blurting out the truth before she could stop herself.

Penelope's eyes filled with tears.

Aunt Verity came up behind Penelope, Tappy still on her shoulder and Marzipan and Horatio scampering at her heels.

"Girls, why don't you stop for ice cream at Sweet Betsy's before Penelope goes home? My treat," said Aunt Verity. "I'll head back to my house with the cats in the car."

"How marvelous! I'd love that!" said Penelope.

"Elsby?" said Aunt Verity.

Elsby twirled her umbrella and looked down at the wet ground. She very much wanted to say *no*. She had made up her mind never to bother with Penelope again.

"What do you think, Elsby?" Aunt Verity said gently. "It would be a nice thing to do."

Elsby sighed. Her wish to not disappoint Aunt Verity outweighed anything else.

"Okay," she mumbled. "I guess I can do that."

Penelope's thick black dress dripped so much rainwater on the tiled floor of the ice cream parlor that the worker handed her a roll of paper towels to mop it up. Elsby didn't offer to help.

While Penelope went to the bathroom to wring out her clothes in the sink, Elsby stood by the door and looked out the big glass window at Roger Williams Street. She was still so angry she couldn't think straight. Sunlight broke through the rain clouds and dipped the street trees' leaves in gold.

Penelope came back and stood by the counter. Elsby felt her glancing her way, but she avoided her gaze and instead stared at the rows of flavors.

"Mint chocolate chip in a sugar cone, please," Penelope said.

"Coffee. In a cup," Elsby mumbled when it was her turn. She was remembering the time Penelope called her naïve. What could be more grown-up than coffee-flavored ice cream in a cup?

Elsby paid for both ice creams with the money Aunt

Verity had given her and followed Penelope to a table by the window.

Elsby took a nibble of the ice cream and couldn't help making a face. Her mother always said "you'll probably love coffee when you're older." Well, maybe Elsby wasn't old enough yet.

"Do you really like coffee ice cream?" asked Penelope, biting her cone.

"No," Elsby said after a pause. She swirled her plastic spoon around the cup. "It's disgusting."

"I'm sorry," said Penelope, taking another bite. "I mean, not just about the ice cream. About everything else. What I did."

Elsby dared to look up. Penelope's eyes were very wide behind her smudged glasses. Stripes of rain-blurred eyeliner ran down her cheeks.

"But why did you make an oath—that was your idea, by the way—and then break it?" asked Elsby. "Why did you leave me out of . . . of everything? *Why?*"

Penelope hunched her shoulders. "I didn't *want* to break it. I didn't *want* to leave you out."

But you *did*, Elsby thought, and bit her lip. It was hard work to keep quiet and listen.

"I just . . . Clarissa snuck over to my house and convinced me that she could help me learn to see ghosts. For my business."

"She *snuck* over to your house?"

Penelope nodded. "Yes. Wearing her ball gown and everything. She climbed up the wall and knocked on my window."

"She told you she could help you see ghosts? But why couldn't you include me?" Elsby asked.

Penelope studied the table. "She told me that if she was going to be helping me, we had to keep it secret from you. That you—that you weren't as special or talented as me."

Elsby flinched.

"She lied," Penelope said, looking up. "Now I know she was really just trying to test me out for her stupid spells." Penelope turned and tossed her half-eaten cone in the garbage can. Then she put her head in her hands. "But it's my fault I went along with it. I'm sorry." She peeked out between her fingers. "Can you just *try* to forgive me?"

Elsby hesitated. Then she nodded. She could try, at least.

Penelope lowered her hands. "The weird thing is, you actually *had* seen a ghost, even though none of us knew it. You were able to see Rose."

Elsby shrugged. She stood up and tossed her cup of coffee sludge in the trash, too. "Not because I wanted to," she said, sitting down again.

"I think Clarissa knew you have a gift. She was afraid you were on to her—that you were suspicious and would figure out what she was really up to." Penelope blushed. "I was too caught up in how much she had flattered me to realize that she was tricking me."

Elsby blinked. Clarissa had only ever been rude to her. But now Elsby tried to imagine how she would have acted if Clarissa had been nice to her. Would she have fallen for Clarissa's lies? Maybe . . . or maybe not. But it was something to think about.

"Everyone makes mistakes," Elsby finally said. It felt very grown-up to say that. Maybe even more grown-up than liking coffee-flavored ice cream.

"I was such a brat, and you came to the Athenaeum to save me anyway," said Penelope. She paused and smiled slyly. "Even though I'm not a cat, or a homeless bunny, or a chicken."

Elsby laughed.

"Maybe someday I can come visit you in New York." Penelope raised her eyebrows. "There has to be a ton of ghosts in that city, considering how many people well . . . die there."

"I actually think it's the exact opposite," said Elsby. She slowly exhaled—she hadn't realized how tightly she'd been holding her breath. "The living crowd them out."

"This calls for an investigation," said Penelope, raising one finger in the air.

Suddenly Elsby remembered Aunt Verity's warnings

against ghost hunting. *There are some nasty things out there, and you must always take care.*

But how did Rose Fairweather fit into all that?

There was so much to figure out.

Elsby touched the amulet at her throat. The salt was gone, but Aunt Verity had managed to wedge the gold lid back into the crystal vial. It still felt like something with power.

"I know," Penelope said quickly, glancing at the amulet. "It's not safe to hunt for ghosts. And after last night, I'm not sure how much I'm interested in exploring that stuff anymore—magic, or anything else."

Elsby and Penelope shuddered in unison.

"But maybe—maybe we could talk to other people who have seen ghosts, and write down what they say, and make it into a book?"

"That sounds so cool," said Elsby, because it did.

"Maybe you can do some interviewing around New York, and we can write to each other about what we find. Do you know that in the olden days people used to close all their letters with globs of melted wax, then press special carved seals into them? I found one at Goodwill with a raven on it and I use it for all my letters. I put them inside another regular envelope. I think it makes the words seem more interesting." Penelope paused. "I promise to send you some letters, if you want?"

"That sounds amazing," said Elsby.

Text messages could never compete with a real wax-sealed letter.

The rain had stopped. Outside it was a hot afternoon, bright and loud with birdsong.

Elsby and Penelope chattered all the way down Roger Williams Street, swinging their umbrellas as they walked to the Bubble Palace, where Penelope's mother was sweeping the sidewalk.

"I have to go load the detergent vending machine," said Penelope with a sigh.

"I wish we could keep hanging out," said Elsby.

The words were out in the open before Elsby could stop them. They came not from her head, but from her heart. Her brain still rumbled a little with thoughts like *she betrayed me* and *I never want to be friends with her ever again.*

But her heart said otherwise.

Just like that, Elsby found she really *had* forgiven Penelope.

"There you are, Penelope!" said her mother, looking across the parking lot with her hand shading her eyes. "The detergent is waiting."

Penelope's shoulders sagged.

"I wish I wasn't going home so soon," said Elsby. Her

mother was coming to fetch her in just two days.

"Me, too. It's the worst!" said Penelope.

"Will you—will you actually write to me?" asked Elsby.

"Yes. I promise. I know you probably don't believe me, but I will. And you'll write back. And we can call each other," said Penelope. "And practice telepathy." She paused and shut her eyes. "Quick, Elsby. What color am I thinking of?"

"Um . . . green?"

Penelope frowned and opened her eyes. "Blue. We're going to have to work on this," she said.

"We will," said Elsby.

Penelope leaned over and pulled Elsby into a hug.

"I'm so glad we met. I'm sorry for everything," said Penelope. "Thank you for saving me."

Elsby watched as Penelope hurried up to the front door of the laundromat, sidestepping puddles on the way. Her mother looked like she was scolding her, but just before going through the glass door, Penelope turned around and waved.

And Elsby waved back.

CHAPTER TWENTY-SIX

The Cats of Silver Crescent

That afternoon Marzipan perched on several carefully balanced cushions on a chair at Aunt Verity's kitchen table. She sipped from the cup of mint tea Elsby had made her and took tiny bites of fresh blueberry pie. Rain drummed down the windowpanes.

"I'm hoping your aunt can help me send my poems out to literary magazines, like Rose did," said Marzipan, primly wiping her mouth with a napkin. She was fully clothed again, this time in a brown and white calico dress under a cream-colored pinafore. "Like with the postage when I need it and printing out the letters. Most of them I can submit on the Internet."

"I'm sure she will. She has a laptop you can borrow, and she must have a printer," said Elsby.

"I don't even need to borrow the laptop. I have Rose's old one. I just need her to give me her Wi-Fi password. I'm actually quite good at typing," said Marzipan.

Elsby put down her fork and giggled at the image of a cat working on a computer.

"But I must read some of *your* work before you go home!" Marzipan smiled.

Home. It seemed too soon. Elsby was excited to see her mother, but she would miss the cats—and Penelope and Aunt Verity, too.

At least Elsby wasn't as anxious as usual about her mother taking an airplane. Somehow the experience with the cats—and Clarissa's diabolical plot—had made the rest of the everyday world seem less perilous.

"Please? Perhaps you could read one of your novels out loud to me," said Marzipan.

"Chapters. Not novels. I've only written first chapters. I can't ever finish anything else," Elsby said, staring down at her own slice of blueberry pie, wishing she had kept her mouth shut from the beginning and never told anyone about her writing. Why was it so embarrassing to talk about?

"A first chapter, then," said Marzipan. "But what's stopping you from writing the second chapter?"

"Well, I can never think of how to make it good. So, I . . . stop."

"You just have to put one word after the other," said Marzipan. "You can always go back and fix things later."

"I guess that's true," said Elsby.

"Of course it's true."

Elsby heard the sound of her aunt's car pulling into the driveway.

"Have Horatio and Tappy made up their minds yet?" Elsby asked Marzipan, eager to change the subject.

Aunt Verity had agreed to adopt the cats, if they so desired, but so far only Marzipan had said she was interested.

"They'll come around to it," Marzipan said, dabbing her lips with her napkin. "They have to, because soon enough those nieces will settle their inheritance fight and we will be out of a home. Tappy weeps whenever I remind her about this."

"Do you think Clarissa will come back?" Elsby asked, lowering her voice.

"I don't know. We discovered she came to the house before she ran away—a small suitcase was missing, along with her favorite clothes and some of the spell books. . . ."

Elsby shuddered.

"Don't worry. I think it will be a long time before she tries anything like that spell again. And certainly not anywhere near here." Marzipan dropped her voice to a whisper. "Your aunt is clearly a great mage."

Elsby's aunt came through the kitchen doorway with a few bags from Roy's. The cats had given her a list. Elsby wondered if the butcher was curious about the sudden popularity of liver.

"I'm not a great mage," Aunt Verity said, smiling and setting down the groceries. "Just gifted in unusual ways. My whole life I have been attempting to get a handle on it."

"You don't . . . you aren't like—" Elsby stopped short. She didn't want to say it out loud, but what if her aunt was just as evil as Clarissa?

"I don't do the kind of nasty magic that Clarissa practiced. Heavens, no!" said her aunt, as though she read Elsby's mind.

Elsby sighed with relief.

"There are many kinds of magic. Some are good. Rose tried to be good, though she got in over her head," Aunt Verity continued.

"She died because of it," murmured Marzipan, and let out a long sigh.

"And some types of magic are very, very, *very* bad. Clarissa's is among the worst. Conjuring the dead! Stealing souls! Abominable." Aunt Verity shook her head. "But all that wickedness will come back to bite Clarissa. It always does."

"But how—how does magic even work?" asked Elsby.

"It's a good question—one for which I have no satisfactory answer. It seems to me quite arrogant to assume we can ever fully understand the workings of the cosmos! Though we should never stop trying."

Elsby squinted. "Are you really an archaeology professor, too? Or is that, like, just a cover?"

"Of course I am! It's hard to make a living as a wizard these days." Aunt Verity smiled. "Not that being a professor is much easier. Though it does give me some flexibility." She sighed. "I always have to move because strange things start happening around me. Even here. How on earth did I manage to rent the only place in town—maybe the world—next door to a bunch of talking cats?" She shook her head.

"Or perhaps it's the other way around," said Marzipan, and then took a prim little sip of tea. "How did our dear Rose manage to rent her property to the only great mage in Snipatuit?"

"Oh, Snipatuit is an odd place," said Aunt Verity. "Even if I were a great mage—and I'm *not*, Marzipan—I feel quite certain that I'm not the only one here."

Later that evening, after Marzipan had gone back to her side of the house to see Horatio and Tappy, after her aunt had made Elsby promise to never sneak out again and then gone to bed, after her mother had called to wish her good night and Elsby wondered how she would explain to her everything that had happened, Elsby sat on her bed in the little attic room. Her notebook was open to a blank page.

You just have to put one word after the other.

Elsby picked a random pencil from her case and wrote:

The Cats of Silver Crescent
Chapter One

She didn't pause to decorate the letters, or sketch a picture, or ponder character names. She could do all of that later. She didn't get up to refill her water glass, or stop to look up a word in her thesaurus, or stare out the window into the darkness.

Instead she just wrote one word after another, until she had filled five whole pages and realized she was at the end of chapter one.

And then Elsby turned the page and began to write Chapter Two.